On the Mystery of Rennes-le-Château

As Sherlock Holmes used to say,
"Once you eliminate the impossible, whatever remains,
no matter how improbable, must be the truth"

From A. Barlow (Guardian 9th January)

© *Julian Doyle UK (22nd May 2023)*

All rights reserved. Apart from any fair dealing for the purposes of research or private study, or criticism or review, as permitted under the Copyright, Designs and Patents Act 1988, this publication may only be reproduced, stored or transmitted, in any form or by any means, with the prior permission in writing of the publishers, or in the case of reprographic reproduction in accordance with the terms of licenses issued by the Copyright Licensing Agency. Enquiries concerning reproduction outside those terms should be sent to the publishers, chippenhamfilms@icloud.com

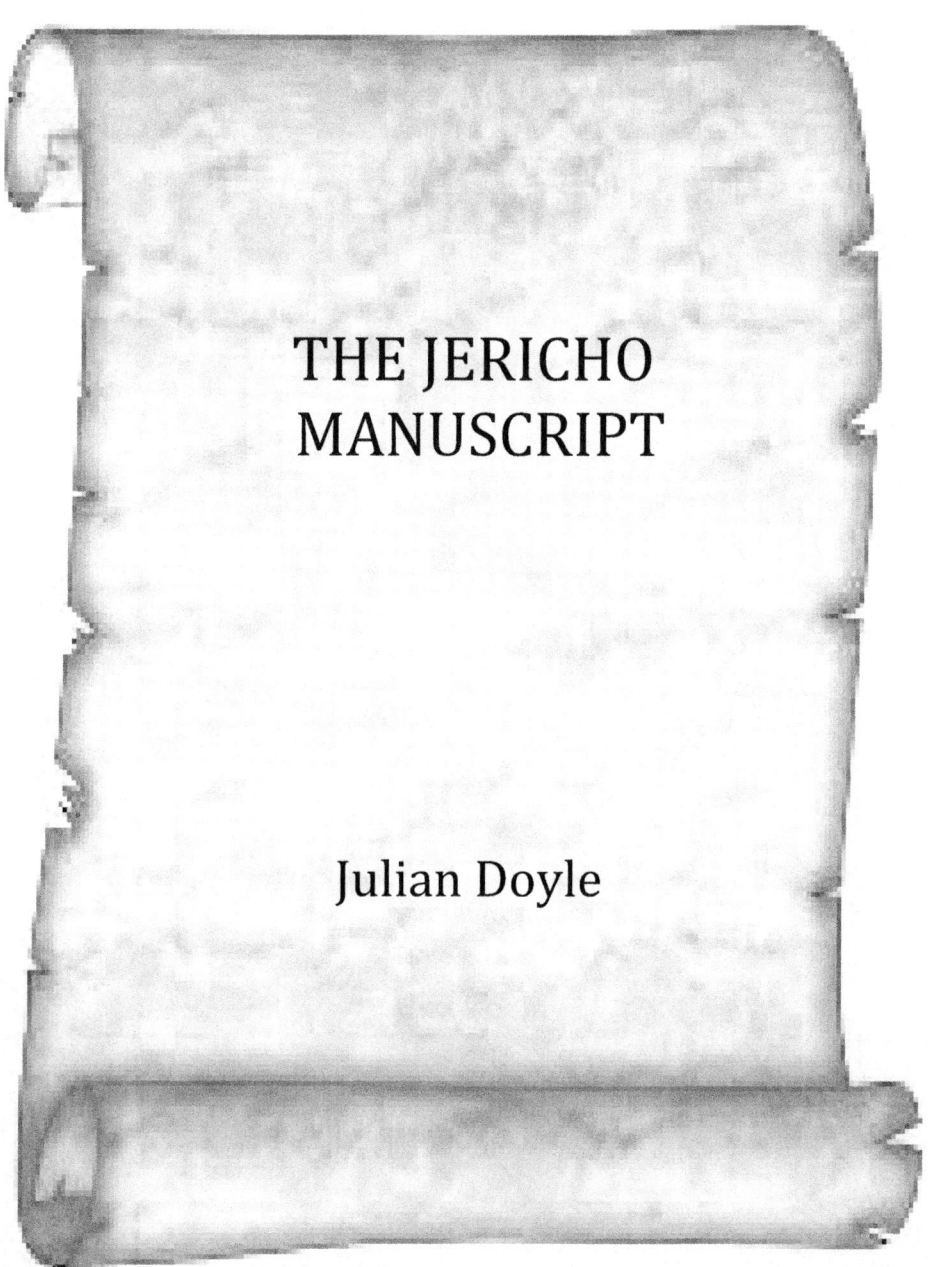

THE JERICHO MANUSCRIPT

Julian Doyle

LETTER FOUND WITH MANUSCRIPT

I have written in full one of the most extraordinary episodes of investigation completed by my friend Sherlock Holmes. But because of the sensitive nature of the material I have instructed that this should not be published for one hundred years after my death. While my friend has no such compulsion, almost dismissing the extraordinary results as elementary. He clearly does not realise the controversial nature of his discoveries, so controversial that it could well lead to attempts on his very person. I cannot even tell my good wife as it would, like many others, disrupt the foundation of her life and attack her very soul.

I cannot imagine the world a hundred years from now. Will the British Empire have spread 'wider still and wider' as Elgar suggests or has the recently united German states threaten to create a new empire. Their victory over the French has puffed them up to be looking for a fight with anyone to show off their new German superiority. Who will be the King of England then, and what type of government will we have? But most importantly, how will these astonishing discoveries made by my friend be accepted in this new world?

Holmes refuses to enter into any discussion concerning the material, he simply says in his usual offhand manner, "it is elementary my dear friend, so others can easily discover the truth for themselves."

So my future reader I place before you the account of the case of Canon Alfred Lilly with nothing removed or edited and I hope it is not so shocking to you as it was to me and would be to any reader in our days.

PUBLISHERS NOTE

This unpublished episode written by Dr. *'James'* Watson of an investigation by *'Stephen'* Holmes was offered to us by Mr. Julian Doyle who was a close friend of Andrew Watson, a relative of the author. The first names of the people involved had been changed, perhaps the author thought removing the first names would be enough in a hundred years to conceal their true identity. But I think we all know who *'Stephen'* and *'James'* really are, so with Mr. Doyle's permission we have used the names of the real people. The Doyles and the Watsons have been close families for many years, and the two friends discovered this account in amongst the mass of Andrew's great grandfather's documents. Andrew Watson was killed last year in a motorcycle accident and as he had no surviving relatives, the copies are now in the sole possession of Julian Doyle. So while it is just 96 years since the writer died, Mr. Doyle approached us with a desire to publish now, for what he says is his own personal safety. The material is still as controversial now, as it would have been then, but we think Mr. Doyle's concerns are probably unwarranted given the author and the detective are both dead.

For your further information we have checked all the Biblical quotes and they are correct and come from the King James translation. The same is true of all the other quotes from the ancient historians, Tacitus, Suetonius and Josephus.

There are some words used in the text, which are now unacceptable. We have not removed them for historical reasons so the text is exactly as Dr. Watson wrote it, including some quaint spelling. There is also mention of quite a few classical paintings, we thought it might be useful to the reader if we added copies of them into the text, something that would have been financially prohibitive one hundred years ago but now adds very little extra costs.

THE ALFRED LILLY AFFAIR

CHAPTER 1

It was Monday the 24th June in the year that Queen Victoria died. I know the day because it is John the Baptist's day, the most important date in the Freemasons calendar, when my friend the Reverend David Adams burst into my house. He had come from the Freemasons dinner via the house of his clerical friend, Canon Alfred Lilly.

"He was not there to preside over events," stammered Adams. "So I went to his house. I have not touched anything. You told me Sherlock Holmes demands he observe the scene of the crime before the police trample on the clues."

"Calm down. What crime are you talking about?"

"I'll tell you in the cab, it's waiting. Grab your coat and let us to Holmes immediately."

I had been together with Adams in the tightest of scrapes in Afghanistan, where he was Chaplin, but he always kept control. Perhaps it had been a façade for the men, but now faced with some dreadful crime alone, he seemed to have lost all composure.

At Bakers Street we picked up Holmes and exchanged our Hansom for a four-wheeler, which headed up the Edgware Road and left down beside the Regent's canal. Adams recounted the story to Holmes who listened without a word, but his eyes told me he was studying every syllable. Just before the Paddington basin we turned right over the canal bridge to the wide expanse of Warwick Avenue with its Georgian stucco fronted buildings unlike any other part of London. Ahead was the majestic St. Saviour's Church at the end.

Adams called to the driver, "Here, left by the door of the rectory."

The cabby brought the horse to a halt at the side of the church and we descended and approached the door.

"It looked closed but the latch had not fallen," said Adams.

"You go first Mr. Holmes, I have touched nothing."

"Step back a moment gentlemen," said Holmes as he examined the front step and then the door lock from both sides. He bent down and removed a crumpled paper from the lower doorpost. It must have caused the door latch not to fall. He then went round the front garden and by the cedar tree he bent down and picked up something with his fingers, smelt it and returned it to where it had been. He paused for a moment and then rose and we followed him into the hall.

"He is in the study to your left," said Adams. "The gas lights were on as you see them".

Holmes entered the room. Ahead was the back of a man slumped over his desk. As Holmes circled him the pool of blood came into view and then the dagger that had been plunged into the side of his neck.

"Was this exactly as you found him?" asked Holmes.

"Exactly. It was obvious that he was dead from the moment I saw the knife and the blood."

Holmes saw something on the ground by the desk. He bent down and lifted it up, it was a length of green ribbon, which he returned back to its place on the floor. He then continued his circle and his thin body, long neck and hooked nose made him look like a vulture examining a carcass. But I knew Holmes was studying every small detail of the scene. From what I could see there was a piece of white paper to the left and a pen, which had splattered ink onto the writing.

"Do you think it is suicide or murder, Mr. Holmes?"

"I will answer that in just a moment." Holmes circled again while we made a wider move to the front.

"Watson, could you find another piece of paper and write down every word written. Don't use the pen on the table and be careful when you dip in the ink not to disturb anything. Don't touch that second, unopened inkbottle, just the open one nearest the body. I will just take a look around the house to see if there are any further clues."

And with that Holmes left Adams and myself to follow his instructions. I found another pen in the drawer and dipped it into the open inkbottle and wrote:

'Mark 10:46. And they came to Jericho and the sister of the youth whom Jesus loved and his mother and Salome were there, and Jes...'

That was it, a quote from Mark's Gospel, which seemed to have no apparent significance to the events that had unfolded. Holmes returned.

"I am afraid that the answer to your question Reverend Adams is that your friend Canon Alfred Lilly has been murdered. The perpetrator was a thin man who took him by surprise. Probably a Mohammedan."

Adams sank back into a nearby chair and looked up at me. I nodded, knowing that feeling he had that Holmes seemed to pluck knowledge out of thin air. Later when he explained to me how he did it, it would just seem so obvious. For now Holmes continued as if he had just said the most mundane of statements. "I see some half un-packed bags in the bedroom, has the deceased been travelling recently?"

Adams nodded, "yes he has been in Paris. He is an expert in ancient languages and was there to complete a translation of a manuscript held at the church of Saint Sulpice."

Holmes wondered for a moment. "Was the Canon a man who might steal such a manuscript?"

"No, of course not," replied Adams indignantly. "Why do you ask such a thing?"

"Because he was making a copy from a rolled up manuscript when he was attacked," said Holmes.

"How do you know that?" asked Adams. "There is no sign of a manuscript."

"That was the purpose of the two inkbottles, they held open the roll while he worked. The green ribbon was used to tie the scroll and was under it, when the scroll was removed it fell to the floor. The fact that the manuscript is missing but nothing else of value, suggests this was the object the murderer was after."

"Goodness me!" exclaimed Adams.

Holmes looked at the written paper and then took my copy and checked that I had written the text correctly. He turned to the Rev. Adams. "Would you know if there are any other references to Jericho in the Gospels?"

"I believe so, in the synoptic Gospels Jesus cures a blind man in Jericho."

"Synoptic Gospels?" asked Holmes.

"The Gospels of Matthew, Mark and Luke are lumped together and called the synoptic Gospels, from the Latin, which means 'seen through one eye.' These synoptic Gospels tell many of the same stories, often in the same words, frequently following the same order. They in fact, were the original Bible and John was added later."

"I see I am very uneducated when it comes to the Bible," admitted Holmes.

Where he was an expert, Holmes talked with arrogant certainty, but he had no qualms about admitting any area which he lacked knowledge. In fact he rather boasted that a man should keep his little brain-attic stocked with all the furniture that he was likely to use, and the rest he should put away in the lumber-room of his library.

"Well there is nothing more for us to learn here," announced Holmes. "We will hand over the investigation to the Police, while I realise I have to invest some serious time in the books of my library before I can take the investigation any further."

CHAPTER 2

The Missing Jericho Manuscript

Two days later, we arrived at Baker Street; Adams was hot with news and followed me carrying his 'Morning Herald.' I took him straight up to where Holmes sat reading. Without turning Holmes welcomed us. "Good morning gentlemen and what is the news that has so excited you Adams?"

Adams was a little taken-a-back, but surprising clients with accurate observations were the norm for my detective friend.

Adams opened the paper. "Yes, have you seen this?"

Holmes smiled. "So what have the Police concluded in the Alfred Lilly case?"

"Because nothing is missing from the house and there is no obvious motive, they have concluded it was suicide." Adams announced.

"They suggest he wrote a passage from the Bible before thrusting the knife into his neck," I added.

"What side of the desk was the pen and paper, Watson?" asked Holmes.

I thought about it, "The left as I remember," then realised what I had said. "Ah yes, so he was left handed."

"Yes Watson. If he was left handed he would slit his throat from right to left, and if he was going to stab his throat with his left hand it would be in the right, not reach up awkwardly to stab the left where we found the knife."

I went through with the actions and Holmes was right. It was very difficult to stab the left with the left hand, much easier to slit your throat from right to left, or stab the right.

"So you suggest a man crept up behind him and stabbed him. A thin man you said."

"Yes."

"How do you know he was thin?"

"The floor was carpeted and when I walked towards Lilly I did it silently. You are both of average size and must weigh a good two stone more than me."

"Yes you are considerably thinner than both of us." I agreed.

"And, you may not have noticed, but when each of you followed me there was a floor board that made quite a creak as each of you stepped on it. Neither of you could have taken Lilly by surprise. He would have been out of his chair and round to you."

Adams looked at me and I shrugged and turned to Holmes. "I must admit, Holmes, I never noticed the noises we made when crossing the floor."

"Furthermore," added Holmes, "he did not write a quote from the Bible."

"But I wrote it myself," I said indignantly.

"Yes I saw him," agreed Adams, "there it is on the table. Mark 10:46."

The Reverend picked up the paper with my writing and read.

"And they came to Jericho and the sister of the youth whom Jesus loved and his mother and Salome were there, and Jes..'

"You may be a man of the cloth my friend but I am afraid that is not Mark 10:46." Holmes handed Adams his Bible, which had a dozen numbered tabs. "Check tab 1."

Adams opened the Bible at tab 1 to find Mark 10. Glancing down to verse 46, he read.

"And they came to Jericho: and as he went out of Jericho with his disciples and a great number of people.

"What do you make of that, Watson?" Holmes asked.

I was puzzled. "I don't know. It started the same but then veered off."

"Read the original again would you Adams."

"And they came to Jericho: and as he went out of Jericho with his disciples -"

Holmes butted in there. "They arrive at Jericho, they leave Jericho, what happened in Jericho? The New Testament would be rather a dull read if it was full of places Jesus went into and out of with nothing happening."

"Are you suggesting there was a cut here?" asked Adams.

"Obviously there was, and the Canon was translating a manuscript that may have come from his work in Saint Sulpice, which was a copy of the cut. So we now know the cut began with, '*and the sister of the youth whom Jesus loved and his mother and Salome were there, and Jes...*' And Jes.. I presume is Jesus who did something with these people; and whatever it was, was deemed by the early church to be unfit for our eyes. A few moments more in Lilly's life and perhaps we could stab a guess at what it was, but now the manuscript is in the hands of the murderer and we just have the eighteen words that one imagines have never ever seen the light of day before."

Adams was horrified, "Surely you must tell all this to the police?"

Holmes placed his fingers together and slowly shook his head. I don't think there is much point, I imagine the murderer made post haste to France and is unlikely to be ever apprehended by our police."

"Why do you think he has fled to France? And, by the way, why did you suggest he is a Mohammedan?"

"The attacker was waiting by the cedar tree and, as you know Watson, I am an expert on tobacco remains. On the floor was a cigarette end, which I identified as strong continental tobacco, most likely from a French Gauloises. And on the table there," he pointed to a scrap of paper, "is the little paper wedge used to stop the door latch from falling. You will see it has a few letters in Arabic.

I unfolded the scrap.

"As yet I have not had it translated, but it is unlikely to yield much as it just looks like a few letters, not even a whole word. There are quite a few Mohammedans in France due to its colonies in North Africa, which again points to France as the assailants place of residence."

"Are we then to give up the chase?" I asked.

"I am afraid I am not up to date with the Bible story to know what we are dealing with. You see from the books on my desk I have been studying all day and most of the night to familiarise myself with the subject, so I can get a complete understanding of the situation. And then, Watson, if your new wife will allow, I would like you to join me on a trip to Paris."

CHAPTER 3

The Mystery of Bethany

Holmes asked me to join him the next day for a visit to the National Gallery where there was an exhibition he was keen to see. We arranged to meet at Charing Cross, appropriately the very centre of London from which all distances to the Capital are measured. I was travelling by Hansom, Holmes was getting there by the new Baker Street and Waterloo Railway, which travelled underground and had been financed by rich cricket fans who complained about the traffic getting to and from Lord's Cricket ground.

I found Holmes sitting on the bench outside the station clutching his Bible.

"How was your journey?" I asked.

"Would you believe, under fifteen minutes," said Holmes.

"That is impressive. It took me twenty five from Queen Ann Street, a far shorter journey."

"You are alone. Good," nodded Holmes.

"Well you did ask me not to bring the Reverend. Since he has offered to pay our expenses it seemed a little harsh to exclude him."

"I do not want him prejudicing my inquiry with church interpretations as opposed to what is actually written. Also I do not feel totally comfortable to discuss some of my findings in his presence if it undermines his position."

I looked at Holmes for more explanation but he was not forthcoming. So I asked about the case and what news he had.

"Nothing as yet about the case, I am still trying to unravel what might have been in the manuscript to see if it gives a clue as to who might be interested enough to kill for it."

"Perhaps it just has a value as an ancient document irrelevant to what it contained," I suggested.

"That could be true, but I don't think so. Already in my reading things are unravelling. Here, sit down, the exhibition does not open for another half hour." Holmes motioned for me to sit next to him. "It is warm enough to spend some time on the bench while I bring you up to date with my investigation." He opened his Bible at one of his tabs. They had grown in number since I last saw his Bible. He was about to read but stopped.

"Wait, before I start I must make something clear about the Jesus story that we all know so well. Unfortunately it is a mix, taking bits from each Gospel to make a coherent account. But like any good procedure we need to keep separate the Gospels and the information they contain because each Gospel has a slightly different approach and one writer appears to have very clear prejudices, and it is important to identify him."

"Very well," I nodded.

Holmes again was about to read but again stopped and took out his notebook. "I should add the details Irenaeus writes about the witnesses…"

"You mean the Gospel writers," I interrupted. "Matthew, Mark, Luke and John."

"Yes for us they are the witnesses to the events. Irenaeus tells us Mark, was an associate of Peter and wrote his Gospel in Rome." Holmes read from his notes.

"Mark, the disciple and interpreter of Peter did hand down to us what had been preached by Peter."

"Luke on the other hand travelled with Paul.
'Luke the companion of Paul, recorded in a book the Gospel preached by him.'

"It is vital that you note that like Paul, Luke never knew Jesus, which he admits when opening his Gospel." Holmes put down his notes and opened a tab on the Bible at beginning of Luke and read.

'Many have undertaken to draw up an account of the things that have been fulfilled just as they were handed down to us. I myself have carefully investigated everything, and have decided to write an orderly account for you.'

"So clearly, as a witness, Luke is rather useless since all his evidence is heresy. He has no personal information for us concerning Jesus. The three original Gospels are, as Adams described them, the synoptic Gospels and Irenaeus writes that John was added later."

'Afterwards, John, the disciple of the Lord did himself publish a Gospel.'"

"With all this in mind let me tell you what I have discovered when I looked up the references to Jericho in the synoptic Gospels."

"I am all ears," I said enthusiastically. But still Holmes did not begin but added another proviso.

"At this point I am not expressing my religious beliefs or otherwise, just following evidence as told in the Gospels."

"Yes, yes." I said, "I appreciate all that. But do put me out of all this suspense."

"Fine here are the references to Jericho. In Mark, verse 10, Jesus is in Jericho. Then verse 11 begins with a trip to Jerusalem." Holmes finally opens his Bible at the tab he originally went for before all the stipulations and read.

"'As they approached Jerusalem and came to Bethphage and Bethany at the Mount of Olives.'

"This suggests Jesus was walking from Jericho to Jerusalem when he passed by Bethany where he instructed his disciples to:

'Go to the village ahead of you, and just as you enter, you will find a colt tied there, which no one has ever ridden. Untie it and bring it here. If anyone asks you, 'Why are you doing this?' say, ' The Lord needs it and will send it back here shortly.'"

Holmes looked up to see if I was following. "And lo and behold they find the donkey and bring it to Jesus."

"And he gets on the donkey," said I completing the event, "and rides to Jerusalem where he is welcomed by cheering crowds who lay palms before him. So Jericho leads to Palm Sunday the first day of Jesus passion week."

"Don't get ahead of us it is just a little more complicated than you imagine. For us sadly at this point it does not say if the three ladies mentioned by Lilly as being in Jericho, travelled with him."

"That is a pity."

"But what is odd is that the donkey story in Mark is word for word the same as the other two synoptic Gospels Luke and Matthew."

"So the evidence is corroborated."

"Perhaps, but there is an odd facet to the Bethany reference in the synopics."

"What is that?" I asked.

"We are never told who lives there. You cannot find the name of the occupants of Bethany anywhere in the synoptic Gospels."

"Is that of importance?" I asked.

"Yes because it all becomes rather curious when one adds where Jesus spent that night after arriving in Jerusalem."

'Where?"

Holmes went back to another tab in his Bible and read. *Matthew 21:17 'And he left them and went out of the city to Bethany, where he spent the night.'*
And Mark agrees that every night of that week they stay in Bethany. And even Luke, who has difficulty spitting out the name Bethany makes it clear where Jesus is staying.
'And every day he was teaching in the temple, but at night he went out and lodged on the mount called Olivet.'

"Why do you say Luke has trouble with Bethany?"

Holmes raised a finger, "You will see as we unravel the events in Bethany."

"Are you suggesting Luke cut out references to Bethany and that is what was in the Manuscript?"

"No because the events in the manuscript occurred in Jericho not Bethany, but I do think the cut in the Jericho manuscript involved the unnamed occupants of Bethany."

"Really!" I exclaimed.

"With this new information, let me return to the journey from Jericho to Jerusalem. The first thing one has to consider now is, did the three women Jesus met in Jericho travel with him to Jerusalem?"

"Remind me who they are?"

"One is the sister of the disciple Jesus loved for which we have no name. Two is his mother and three is Salome."

"I think Salome is his...."

"Stop! Don't tell me, I know it is not the dancer of the seven veils. This is why I did not want Adams here. I want to have a clear mind and find out for myself.

"Fine, fine. My lips are sealed."

"Now, obviously I can't go to Palestine and walk from Jericho to Jerusalem, which would have been normal if the events were in England, so I looked on a map and found that Jerusalem is nearly twenty miles from Jericho, which is extraordinarily, some 800 feet below sea level. A traveller walks up hill to Jerusalem, which is a tiring, 2500 feet above sea level: an overall rise of over 3,000 feet. I think we can assume that if Jesus and his entourage made this tiring journey they stopped somewhere overnight. The likely place is where they spend all the following nights, Bethany. But the synoptic Gospels make it sound like they travel from Jericho to Jerusalem in one day and that they just happen to pass by Bethany and magically pick up a donkey, and journey on to Jerusalem and then turn back to stay the night in Bethany! Surely they would stop at their un-named friends house in Bethany to tell them that they will be back later to spend the night. And every other night of that week."

I considered this. "Yes that does seem likely."

"But this was the Bible story till John was added to the New Testament. And as I read John last, I was suddenly surprised that we get the names of the occupants of Bethany in the very first reference to the place in John. He opened a new tab.

"Now a man named Lazarus was sick. He was from Bethany, the village of Mary and her sister Martha."

This is the beginning of the raising of Lazarus and there is a clear indication of Jesus close relationship to this family. *'Now Jesus loved Martha and her sister and Lazarus."*

"Why are they not named in the synoptic Gospels?" I asked.

"I have no idea," replied Holmes. "There then follows a second visit to Bethany when Mary anoints Jesus with expensive oils with her hair. Jesus stays the night and then, lo and behold, the next morning he gets on a donkey and rides into Jerusalem!"

I grasped the implication, "So we have, as you already suspected, Jesus not travelling from Jericho to Jerusalem and happening to pass Bethany but staying the night there."

"Exactly, and no longer do we have the magical discovery of a donkey," added Holmes. "But instead we find he just: *'found a young donkey and sat on it.'* So no magical instructions at all and one must ask, which is the most likely version?

"Well…"

"And remember," interrupted Holmes, "prior to John's Gospel being added, Lazarus, Martha and Mary were not mentioned, as living in Bethany, so the magical donkey version would appear more believable. Now it is obvious who must own the donkey. Perhaps this explains why there was reluctance by some to include John's Gospel, as he seems to deflate the whole donkey story and bring it down to earth."

"It is rather damning evidence. I can see why you wanted to exclude Adams from our discussion?"

"No there is worse, said Holmes seriously. "You just told me what happened when Jesus entered Jerusalem riding on the donkey."

"The triumphal entry." I exclaimed. "Yes, it is in every picture book, the streets crowded with cheering crowds as Jesus rides to the Temple, where he dismounts and overthrows the tables of the money-changers."

Holmes smiled enigmatically. "That is the story you are told is in the Gospels, but is it?"

"Is it not?"

"Let us start with Mark's Gospel.
Jesus entered Jerusalem and went into the temple courts. He looked around at everything, but since it was already late, he went out to Bethany with the Twelve.'
"Where are the cheering crowds? Where are the moneylenders? Where are the Hosannas? Luke tells us.
'They brought the colt to Jesus, threw their cloaks on it and put Jesus on it. As he went along, people spread their cloaks on the road. When he came near the place where the road goes down the Mount of Olives, the whole crowd of disciples began joyfully to praise God in loud voices for all the miracles they had seen: "Blessed is the king who comes in the name of the Lord!"

"So are you saying, it is the disciples who are the crowd praising God?" I asked.

"Obviously, they are the ones who can cheer *'for all the miracles they had seen'* not the residents of Jerusalem. This is happening when he first gets on the donkey in Bethany, which John tells us was *'two miles from Jerusalem.'* In fact there is such a place a few miles out of Jerusalem called today in Arabic, 'al-Eizariya', which translates as the *'place of Lazarus.'* So we are talking about twelve disciples, the Bethany family, Lazarus, Mary and Martha, which makes at least fifteen people surrounding Jesus on the donkey. In fact when this crowd of disciples enter Jerusalem, Matthew tells us: *"When Jesus entered Jerusalem, the whole city was stirred and asked, "Who is this?"* So in this Gospel the population of Jerusalem are not cheering the miracles they had seen, they are just confused about who this person is who comes riding into town with a crowd of followers. Not one single Gospel present us with cheering crowds in the streets of Jerusalem, but you have been told it was a triumphal entry."

I thought about this for a moment. "This rather explains something that has always puzzled me."

"What is that?" asked Holmes.

"Why five days later, these same people who cheered his entry as a King of the Jews, call for his crucifixion as a criminal. But now you tell me there were no cheering crowds, just cheering disciples."

"A good point, Watson. Furthermore only one Gospel states that on that same day Jesus turned over the tables of the moneychangers. One has it on the following day after spending the night in Bethany and John's Gospel contradicts them all by stating that the turning of the tables occurred two years earlier at the beginning of his ministry just after turning the water into wine."

"My head is spinning," I admitted. "This is all too much to take in."

"I must confess I hardly slept last night as it unfolded," said Holmes.

We sat for a moment in silence. Somehow in ten minutes and using just a trip from Jericho to Jerusalem, Holmes had brought more interesting individuality to the four Gospel writers than I had from all the many hours I had spent sitting in church pews.

Suddenly Holmes tucked his Bible under his arm and stood up. "So that is a day in the life of Jesus and I presume the manuscript Lilly was translating was about events on the previous day."

If that was what Holmes did to one day in the life of Jesus, I wondered what on earth he would make of the other seven hundred days of His ministry, if he cared to confront them.

Holmes though was off. "Let us cross over to see the exhibition of religious art at the National Gallery."

I jumped up and followed.

"It could be very educational," he added, "to see how artists portray the scenes I am reading about."

CHAPTER 4

The Funny Painting

We crossed William IV Square towards the steps of the National Gallery. Of course Holmes corrected me.

"How can you still call it William IV Square with that massive column to remind you of the name change?"

"I have trouble," I admitted, "calling a square in London by a Spanish name."

"Come on Watson, the name Trafalgar is already almost as British as roast beef."

Holmes was right but as a creature of habit, I do dislike name changes, especially streets even if the new names are in a good cause.

The sun reflected fiercely off the white façade of the National Gallery and as we stepped into the gloom our eyes needed a moment to adjust. Holmes headed straight for the exhibition and paid the thruppence each to enter. He moved swiftly from painting to painting stopping at one or two to identify the scene or to read the sign when he was not sure. But he seemed to be able to identify most scenes.

"So many are of Jesus' birth and death," he commented, "with so few showing the scenes in his life, especially the ones I am interested in."

He stopped abruptly at a painting of Christ crowned with thorns.

"Now that one is interesting," he announced. What do you make of that Watson?"

I read the label out loud, "'*Hieronymus Bosch - Christ Mocked 1520.*' Jesus certainly seems rather calm in the face of these brutal tormenters."

"Anything else?"

"There is something odd about it." I mused. "The clothes, the hats specially, and the iron glove and belted leather collar. I am sure your acute method of observation will bring out more than I can see."

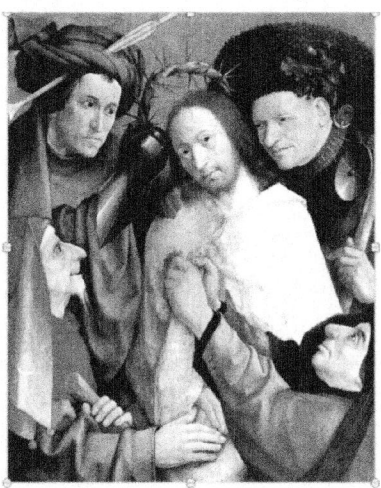

I was never so right because Holmes began a description that left me breathless.

"I would say these are the four human types who surround Jesus, they also represent the four elements, earth, air, fire and water, each associated with the relevant astrological part of the body."

Holmes pointed to the character top right.

"Air, with a stave to thrust Jesus up into the air and touching the shoulder, the very part of the body associated with the air sign Gemini. Fire, the choleric, with iron fist, the metal of Mars that rules over Aries, associated with the head, on which he thrusts the crown of thorns. Water, the phlegmatic type with lewd gesture towards Jesus genitals, linked to the Zodiacal Scorpio, the water sign that rules over the sexual organs. Then Earth, the melancholic, who pulls Jesus down into the dark earth of the grave. The concept of earth, air, fire and water has been all pervasive since Plato coined the phrase 'the four elements.'"

"Holmes!" I gasped. "Don't tell me you are also an expert on paintings."

"Not at all," he smiled. "I am an expert of observation; of paintings I know absolutely nothing. I could not tell you the style of this painting. The country of origin; in fact I only know when it was painted because you read the label."

I remembered Holmes' brother, telling me about their grandmother when we were investigating the Greek Interpreter case. "Now Holmes, Mycroft told me your grandmother was the sister of the French artist Vernet."

"Yes indeed, but while she taught me French she said very little about painting, except that nothing is on the canvas by accident. In this respect it is not like a photograph that can catch accidently a glass of water on the table behind the sitter. If there is such a glass in a painting, the artist has chosen to put it there. So I can just tell you what my eyes actually see and relate it to my knowledge. For instance I see the staff held by Air, will form a cross with the staff held by Water somewhere out here below the canvas." He indicates the crossing point of the two staves. "And I could expand on the significance of the cross in our culture all without knowing a thing about the art of painting."

I shook my head, the man never ceased to amaze me. I watched him move on passing many canvasses as if he was looking for a specific image. He stopped at a painting of Jesus seated being anointed by a lady using her hair.

"No he has it wrong," announced Holmes.

He moved on and found, what I was later to find out was the Burlington House cartoon by Leonardo. It meant nothing to me then but I was later to consider it vitally important to our investigation. Holmes was studying it and the title description. Again he shook his head suggesting there was something wrong with the painting.

On the other side of the room I noticed a small group around the famous painting of the 'Virgin of the Rocks' and pointed it out to Holmes.

"Look there is the Leonardo Da Vinci."

He crossed over and we joined the group of awe inspired spectators. It certainly was an impressive canvas.

"What does it say on the label," asked Holmes.

I bent forward and read: *'Leonardo received the brief in 1483 from the Confraternity of the Immaculate Conception, a brotherhood of Franciscan monks, elected to promote the Vatican's doctrine that Jesus mother was also born of a virgin. The reed cross and Halo were added later to identify the babies as Jesus and John."*

Holmes burst out laughing uncontrollably. He looked away from the painting to try to stop laughing but when he looked back it set him off again. The spectators looked round censoriously.

"What is so funny," I asked.

He looked away to control his laughter.

"What immaculate conception is Leonardo talking about?"

"What do you mean?"

He pointed, "Look at the painting Watson."

I looked; I could see nothing comical at all. "What?"

He set me aside and whispered. "The hole with the rock! Is that not the most phallus looking thing you have ever seen? And as if to emphasise the point, the betrothal arum lily with an exaggerated male stamen at her feet."

I looked, of course the rock appeared through the hole as a large phallus. Was it part of Leonardo's famed sense of humour? Were the rocks by the pool, God's hand? I am ashamed to say the thoughts that passed my mind are not repeatable. I pulled Holmes away to the relief of other spectators and we scampered to the tearoom like naughty schoolboys.

I poured and Holmes added the milk. They make an excellent cup of tea at the gallery if you are ever passing. As we sipped ours I queried Holmes, "You seem to be searching for some specific painting?"

"There are two events that take place in Bethany, the anointing of Jesus feet and the raising of Lazarus. And I am also interested in a moment in the Last Supper. Let me show you how each Gospel handles the anointing." He opens his Bible and flicks open a tab and reads.

"John 12. Jesus came to Bethany, where Lazarus lived, whom Jesus had raised from the dead. Here a dinner was given in Jesus' honour. Martha served, while Lazarus was among those reclining at the table with him. Then Mary took about a pint of pure nard, an expensive perfume; she poured it on Jesus' feet and wiped his feet with her hair.'

"So according to John, this event is happening in Bethany, and it is Mary, one of the women of the house who is doing the anointing. That appears to be pretty conclusive, that is until you read Luke's Gospel." He turns to an earlier tab and reads:

Luke 7:36 'Jesus went to the Pharisee's house and reclined at the table. A woman in that town who lived a sinful life learned that Jesus was eating at the Pharisee's house, so she came there with an alabaster jar of perfume. As she stood behind him at his feet weeping, she began to wet his feet with her tears. Then she wiped them with her hair, kissed them and poured perfume on them. When the Pharisee who had invited him saw this, he said to himself, "If this man were a prophet, he would know who is touching him and what kind of woman she is—that she is a sinner."

"Well that throws a spanner in the works, the only thing these two Gospels agree on is the expensive perfume being poured on the feet and wiped with the hair. On all other counts we are left with just one choice, which witness do we actually believe, John or Luke? Surely the woman anointing Jesus is not a sinner from the city, she is, Mary, the woman of the house as is stated again in John when introducing the raising of Lazarus." Another tab is opened.

"John 11:1 'Now a certain man was sick, Lazarus of Bethany, the village of Mary and her sister, Martha. It was the Mary who anointed the Lord with ointment, and wiped His feet with her hair, whose brother Lazarus was sick.'

So why has Luke suggested it is not Mary but a sinner from the city? Luke admits he never knew Jesus and has no original material about him, but chooses to suggest a sinner from the city did the anointing, which is not in any of the other three Gospels. Here is my plot of the anointing." Holmes opens his notebook and I studied the chart.

GOSPEL	WHO	PLACE	HOUSE OF
John	Mary	Bethany	Lazarus-sisters
Mark	Woman	Bethany	Simon the Leper
Matthew	Woman	Bethany	Simon the Leper
Luke	Sinner	?	Simon the Pharisee

Holmes continued. "So where did Luke get this information about a sinner from the city? Did he read in a source we have no knowledge of, or did he just invent it? If so why blacken the character of the anointer? And what is his problem with Bethany that he seems unable to name the place when all the others agree it is the village where the anointing took place. Can we also agree that, if this is Bethany then it is the house of Lazarus and his sisters? So who is the leper called Simon that the synoptics suggest is the owner? Surely if he is a leper why would anyone go to dinner there?"

"So what is your hunch, because I know you have one? You always do."

Holmes smiled. "Yes I do, I think John is correct and the text of Mark and Matthew has been doctored to remove the name of the owner of the house, which as specified in John's Gospel, is Lazarus."

"Why would they cut out Lazarus' name? It appears a pointless exercise"

"I agree, but it may surprise you that all three Synoptic Gospels have no trace of Lazarus who was clearly an important follower of Jesus.

I was surprised, "Lazarus is not in the synoptic Gospels?"

No, not a whisper. Lazarus is never ever mentioned, which certainly makes him, what we would call, 'a leper' when it comes to the synoptic Gospels."

"But why?" I queried.

"That is the question. Why? What has Lazarus done that he needed to be removed from the synoptic Gospels?"

"You seem very certain that he was removed as opposed to forgotten?"

"Yes I am." Holmes opened his notebook. "This is from Luke: *'Jesus went to the Pharisee's house and reclined at the table...'*
And this is from Mark: *'While Jesus was in Bethany, reclining at the table...'*
So we have Jesus reclining at the table but then when we add the Gospel of John we find: *'Martha served, while Lazarus was among those reclining at the table with Him.'*
So you see the word recline used in all four, but in the three synoptics the person Jesus is reclining with, has disappeared! Surely we are either looking at collusion between the witnesses to remove Lazarus or one of the synoptic writers has doctored the other two."

"And it is already becoming obvious who you think the culprit is," I added. "Luke."

"Yes, but what is missing is any motive."

We finished the tea in silence, I trying to get my head around all this information while Holmes fingered through his Bible. Then swilling back the last drop of tea he stood up. "Come let us see what we can find."

"What is it you are actually looking for?" I asked as I gulped my tea down.

"For a painting of this moment in John 22:
Jesus said, "Most assuredly, I say to you, one of you will betray me." Then the disciples looked at one another, perplexed about whom He spoke. Now there was leaning on Jesus' bosom one of His disciples, whom Jesus loved. Simon Peter therefore motioned to him to ask who it was of whom He spoke. Then, leaning back on Jesus' breast, he said to Him, "Lord, who is it?'
This, I think links up with this description of the anointing.
'She stood behind him at his feet, weeping, and began to bathe his feet with her tears and to dry them with her hair. Then she continued kissing his feet and anointing them with the ointment'.

"Why? What is so important about these two scenes?" I asked as we headed back to the exhibition down a long corridor.

"If the paintings cannot portray them correctly then it suggests the Gospel are documenting real events," answered Holmes, his voice echoing through the corridor.

I had no idea what he was talking about but at least I knew what the quest was and we soon found several paintings of the Last Supper but while they had everyone seated there was no disciple leaning on Jesus bosom. Then passing into another salon we finally found a painting depicting the moment. It showed all twelve disciples seated at the table with Judas slinking in the background, but one of the disciples was a young boy asleep on Jesus bosom.

"Huh!" Holmes announced with glee. "You see it is not possible."

"Here they make him a boy asleep on Jesus lap. But he is supposed to be in conversation with Peter. Can you see what this means?"

I puzzled, "No not really."

"Take a look at that painting of the anointing."

We crossed the room to the painting of Mary before the seated Jesus wiping his feet with her hair.

"You see what is wrong, Watson?"
"No."
"It said she stood behind him."

"Oh yes." I remembered. "But how can she stand behind him and wipe his feet with her hair?"

"How indeed, and how can the disciple recline on Jesus bosom?"

He looked at me questioningly. I was baffled by his question but he did not help me out, he just waved his fingers towards himself, trying to draw the answer out of my mouth. He smiled raising his eyebrows teasing me.

"Think Roman," he said as some sort of clue. At first nothing then suddenly it dawned on me.

"Aahhh. Like a Roman banquet they are lying on sofas."

"Yes! Yes, of course. Lying down he can recline on Jesus bosom. Lying down she can deal with his feet from behind. My hunch was right the painters were unable to depict the events of the Last Supper because they had Jesus and the disciples sitting on chairs."

I shook my head. "You realise Holmes, you have just made all the paintings of the Last Supper null and void."

"Not at all, there are anachronistic detail in many religious painting. Look there at the Holy family, Joseph has glasses. And you see that one of a woman reading."

"Without looking at the label we know who she is because she is wearing green and has a jar at her feet."

"Mary Magdalene?" I guessed.

"Yes. She is usually pained in green or red. This Magdalene is very pale for a middle eastern lady, like someone from northern climes with the local dress, and she is reading a book, which obviously was not yet invented."

I looked at the label, "The Magdalene Reading' by Roger van der Weyden 1399-1464."

"So having chairs is not so damning," added Holmes. "But it does tell us something important."

"What's that?" I asked.

"I have heard some people suggest the whole Jesus story was invented in Rome."

"And this suggests otherwise?"

"Yes, of course," said Holmes confidently. "If the church misinterpreted the text, then the text must have come first."

I considered this, "So you think the fact that the text contradicts the accepted image, suggests it was written independently."

"Yes; there may be cuts and insertions," said Holmes, "but at the base the Gospels are documenting some real events, which means the evidence can be treated like any present day investigation."

"I don't quite follow your logic," I said. "But let's leave it there, I am getting very confused."

"You know Watson, I never expected this to be such an exhilarating investigation," enthused Holmes.

We left the National gallery, Holmes in buoyant mood; his brain activated by the chase, while my brain was still spinning wildly. I had never visited an art gallery and come away so mentally exhausted.

CHAPTER 5

The Rabbi

Two days later we were on the Continental Express from Victoria station heading for Dover. I must admit that I was pleased the affluent Reverend Adams had offered to pay our expenses, as my bank balance would certainly not support such an adventure. I had packed several changes of clothes, while later I found Holmes had packed several changes of books, which explained the trouble we had getting his suitcase on to the luggage rack. I sat by the window watching the Kent hop farms sped by, with their distinctive conically shaped oast houses. They were a new feature to the landscape since the brewing industry expanded as local brewers met the demands of the Navy at Chatham and Deal. Holmes sat next to me reading. Opposite by the window sat a Hebrew in full costume, tangled black hair and a full beard. He wore a blue and white shawl over his shoulders and dangling from his belt was a set of tassels. I assumed our fellow traveller was a Rabbi. I smiled as Holmes was reading the New Testament and by contrast our Rabbi was reading the Old.

We pulled into Canterbury and our carriage filled. A woman sat next to our Rabbi, which seemed to make him most uncomfortable. As the train pulled out he leaned forward and tapped Holmes on the knee. Holmes glanced up from his studies and the Rabbi leaned into his ear and whispered. "Would you like to sit at the window? I should move for my beliefs." Holmes was only too glad to exchange for the window seat opposite me and the exchange was completed with a degree of unsteadiness as the train gathered speed. I wondered if Holmes understood the Rabbi's request, but as a doctor to several Jews I knew. Our Rabbi needed to move for the very delicate reason, in case the woman was at her time, which is one of the things that is unclean for a Jew.

At that moment Holmes leaned forward and tapped the Rabbi on the knee and I suddenly had a dread that Holmes might ask, why the change of seat, which would undoubtedly embarrass the lady. But luckily it was not about that which Holmes wanted to talk about. Having done the Rabbi a favour he felt he could impose on him with some questions.

"Sir, would you mind telling me something about the Passover meal?"

"The Seder?" said the rabbi. "What would you like to know?"

"I read that at a Passover meal one participant broke bread and dipped it. It seemed unlikely."

"Unlikely yes," said the Rabbi.

"Pray tell me why you think so?"

"Certainly. Several days before the Seder our women start removing all the Chometz."

"Chometz?" queried Holmes.

"Any food containing yeast. So not a crumb of bread must be in the house, and the following eight days the household must remain free of 'Chometz'. So the idea that they parted *bread* and dipped it, is as you say, unlikely. Unleavened bread or Matzos are useless to dip and parting it would just snap into pieces. They are clearly talking about ordinary bread which is not allowed at the Seder."

"Another thing that struck me as unlikely is that they ate *'bread'* representing the body and drank wine representing *blood*! Would that not be grotesque to you at the Passover meal as you religiously bleed all your meat?"

"Yes, very true. And glasses of wine serve a particular part in the story represented at the Seder meal. It tells of the time in Egypt when we were slaves and were not allowed to rest while we drank. So at the Seder when you drink wine, you recline. At my house there is a small pillow placed to the left for us to rest while we sip to show we are now free."

"So asking one of your race to drink wine representing blood at the Seder would be unthinkable."

"I think you could say that," replied the Rabbi.

"Thank you, that is most informative." Holmes was clearly dismantling the versions told in the Gospels about the Last Supper. And even more shocking, raising a question over the Eucharist, a standard practice of Church ritual.

"Oh, one other thing," added Holmes. "If you don't mind?"

"No at all."

"What do you think of a group of men leaving the women to go to an empty room to eat the Seder, as you call it?"

"Again it is unlikely. It is not a male only event; it is an important family meal. It requires a lot of preparation, which is done by the women. Lots of small plates of specific foods that tell the story. The meal always follows the same pattern and ends with us singing the Hallel Psalms."

Holmes thanked the Rabbi and sank back in his chair with a contented grin. I could almost feel the cogs of his brain come to a satisfied rest. But not for long because he suddenly swished open his Bible and started flicking through later pages. All his tabs were in the four Gospels but now he was searching in Paul's letters. I noticed him homing in on Corinthians. He pulled out a new tab and stuck it in *1 Corinthians 11:23.*

CHAPTER 6

The Sloop Inn

At Dover instead of embarking we took rooms in the Sloop Inn. After we placed our bags in the room I was expecting to tuck into a fish dinner but Holmes tore a page from his notebook and gave it to me.

"Here is a list of three shipping agents for you and I have four. We need to check if someone with an Arabic name ending in *'zare'* travelled out on the 25th June or 26th. It could be Alazare or Elazare and he was probably travelling with French Papers. Inform them that it is in connection with the murder of Canon Alfred Lilly in London and they should respond favourably."

"Where did you get the name *'zare'* from?" I asked.

"Remember the scrap of paper with the Arabic writing? I had it translated and it offered us these four letters, which I am hoping was part of the murderer's name.

It was nine by the time I returned successfully and I was famished. Holmes was sitting in the parlour of the Sloop smoking his pipe. I removed all expression from my face so I could surprise Holmes with my good news.

"Ah," said Holmes. "You have had some good news."

I should have known I could not fool him.

"How do you know?"

"Your face was too expressionless while your eyes revealed a degree of excitement. Remember the eyes are the windows to the soul. They rarely lie."

"One day, Holmes..."

Holmes smiled then went straight back to business.

"So?"

"Zare was not part of his name it was part of his address. 66, Rue de Lazare. His name was very Arabic, Mohamed Elmeny and he travelled back to France on the 25th. I have his passport number. He had landed in England four days earlier on the 21st."

"Well done, Watson. That is far more than I expected. You have earned a fine dinner, which I see is the reward you most desire."

By that point I did not want to know how Holmes knew, I just wanted that piping hot dinner on the table in front of me.

CHAPTER 7

Aboard the Steam Ship

The channel was flat like a millpond as the steamship throbbed towards Calais. It was warm enough to sit on deck. Holmes opened his suitcase and pulled out a book.

"I think I have exhausted the Bible, I am now going to tackle the books of Josephus. And I wonder if I could impose on you to glance through two books for me. The Roman historians, Tacitus and Suetonius' book 'The Twelve Caesars.' Not all twelve just look at four, Tiberius, Caligula, Claudius and Nero. Look for anything that mentions Jesus or Christians, or for that matter Jews, as the first Christians would be Jews who worshipped like Jesus at the Jewish Temple."

He handed me Tacitus. For himself he took out two books. One was just a torn half.

"Holmes, what have you done to that book?" I gasped.

"This one," said Holmes, holding up the full book, "is Josephus 'Jewish War' book, which covers from Herod the Great to the final action of the War, the siege of Masada in 73 AD. This other piece is part of his second book, 'Antiquity of the Jews' written some twenty years later, it is the whole history of the Jews from Adam and Eve to the start of the War in 66 AD. It is a massive tome from which I am only interested in the end part that overlaps the 'War' book, so I can compare the events. That is why I committed this dreadful act of vandalism on such a precious book. I could not carry the whole thing so I took a knife and spliced off these few pages towards the end.

He was about to close his case when I interrupted the process. "Before you put away the Bible, tell me what you made from your interrogation of the Rabbi aboard the train?"

"Interrogation? That is a bit strong, Watson."

"Done in the gentlest of manners," I added "but as acute as any Scotland Yard grilling."

Holmes smiled as he retrieved his Bible.

"John's Gospel does not say where the Last Supper happened, he just announces when it happened:

John 13:1. Now before the Feast of the Passover when Jesus knew his time had come...'

And then he goes strait into *'During Supper...'* But the synoptic Gospels have a whole new story about where the meal is taking place.

'Luke 22:7 starts with 'Jesus sent Peter and John, saying, "Go and prepare the Passover for us." They said to him, "Where will you have us prepare it?" He said to them, "Behold, when you have entered the city, a man carrying a jar of water will meet you. Follow him into the house that he enters and tell the master of the house, 'The Teacher says to you, Where is the guest room, where I may eat the Passover with my disciples?' And he will show you a large upper room furnished; prepare it there." And they went and found it just as he had told them, and they prepared the Passover. And when the hour came, he reclined at table, and the apostles with him.'

"Mark has the same story, but I must admit this sounds to me very similar to the story of how they magically got the donkey on the way from Jericho, trying to suggest Jesus did not enter Bethany, when we know he spent the night there

"Surely you cannot just go to an empty room and eat the Passover meal, as the Rabbi said, it requires a lot of preparation. My hunch is that the Last Supper, is happening in Bethany and Mary, Martha and Lazarus are present."

"Surely you must have more grounds than that to contradict the Gospels." I complained.

Holmes opened his notebook. "Yes, I do. Unbelievably, it is accidently admitted in an early church document I found. In attempting to downgrade women, the *'Apostolic Church Order'* makes a huge mistake.

"'*When the Master blessed the bread and the cup, and assigned them with the words, this is my body and blood, he did not offer them to the women who are with us. Martha said: "He did not offer them to Mary because he saw her laugh.'*

"In their desperation to attack, they have admitted both Mary and Martha are at the Last Supper. Mind you it is almost impossible to believe they were not present, as Jesus has been staying every night in their Bethany house for the last five days. So why would he up sticks and go to an empty room in Jerusalem for Passover?

"Let me tell the story how I see it, but remember this is un-provable it is just speculation on my part, but it must be considered if we are searching for any episode that required removal."

"So you are just theorizing."

"Yes, my hypothesis goes like this: the following event, I think, is happening the day before Passover.

'Martha had a sister called Mary, who sat at the Lord's feet listening. But Martha was distracted by all the preparations that had to be made. She came to him and asked, "Lord, don't

you care that my sister has left me to do the work by myself? Tell her to help me!" (Luke 10:38)

'*All the preparations that had to be made*' does not sound like doing the washing up. It sounds to me like the preparations for the Passover meal mentioned by the Rabbi, which not only involves preparing all the various symbolic dishes, but cleansing the house, making it absolutely clean of yeast. Then the next day at Bethany the meal begins with Jesus washing the feet of his disciples. He then reclines down on the couch with Lazarus. In response, Mary brings a jar of perfume and she wipes Jesus feet with it. They eat the meal and after we get this little puzzle in John 13. '*When Judas had taken the bread, he went out. And it was night.*' Oddly, turn the page and we have this: '*Judas (not Iscariot) said to him, "Lord, how is it that you will reveal yourself to us, and not to the world?"* Another Judas? Who could it be since we are given the names of the disciples in Matthew and there is only one Judas, the one who betrays him? Something has happened that is vitally important because they have accidentally left in the Bible the name of someone who seems to have been cut everywhere else."

"Who is this second Judas?"

"I have a theory but I will hold fire till I have more information."

"So, you are going to leave me in suspense? Anyway, go on."

"After the meal and the singing of the Passover hymns they go out into the garden, to an olive pressing area, which is the meaning of the word Gethsemane. Judas returns to the garden in Bethany, not you will notice, to the room in Jerusalem and Jesus is arrested. I am convinced the Last Supper, is happening in Bethany and Mary, Martha and

Lazarus are present. And I am beginning to believe that the Bethany family are part of the Jericho cut that we are searching for. Certainly Lazarus we know has been cut from the synoptic Gospels. And secondly it is not clear who the sister of Lazarus and Martha is."

"The sister of Martha is Mary," I confirmed.

"Yes, but Mary who? The church says it is a person called Mary of Bethany," said Holmes. "But I have my doubts. Remember the painting of the Magdalene in the National?"

"Yes."

"Every painting of Mary Magdalene I have ever seen, whether as a saint or as a sinner, always show her with the alabaster jar. That seems the age-old convention when painting the Magdalene, to give her red hair, a green or red dress but always with the alabaster jar to anoint Jesus in Bethany."

"Maybe the painters got it wrong," I suggested.

"This has nothing to do with the painters; they didn't come up with these conventions; it was the early church who commissioned the work and you can be sure if the painter had left out the alabaster jar, the commissioning church would have sent the painting straight back."

""The whole Magdalene story seems very confused," I said.

"Purposefully. And sections about the Magdalene have been cut."

"How do you know that?" I asked.

"Take Mark's Gospel," he opened a tab towards the end of Mark. "There is no mention of the Magdalene then suddenly we get this at the crucifixion. *'There were also women looking on afar off: among whom was Mary Magdalene.'* No introduction at all just a sudden appearance. And this is followed after His death with: "*Now when Jesus was risen early the first day of the week, he appeared first to Mary Magdalene, out of whom he had cast seven devils.*" Mark was a stand alone Gospel yet he suddenly mentions '*the casting out of seven devils*' that is not in his Gospel. There are clearly two possibilities, either he did mention this event earlier and it was cut."

"Yes. What is the other possibility?"

"The description of the casting out of seven devils comes from Luke 8, so it is possible that Luke added this ending into Mark. That would again suggest that Luke not only cut Lazarus out, but then led a character assassination on his sister, which the church continued by replacing her with Mary of Bethany, and then calling the Magdalene a prostitute.

"That is the common consensus about the Magdalene."

"There is nowhere in the Bible that says she is a prostitute," said Holmes angrily, "just that seven devils were removed, which suggests an exorcism."

"Calm down Holmes, I am only repeating what is commonly believed."

"Well 'what is commonly believed' is slander against a person who is not here to defend themselves. And the slander is of the most despicable nature because one Pope, Pope Gregory declared the 'seven demons' were in fact the seven deadly sins of pride, envy, gluttony, greed, lust, sloth and wrath and heaped all these seven sins on to her. So this Pope had pronounced Mary Magdalene to be a fat, greedy, lazy, jealous, angry, prostitute! You can see that the church show no restraint when it comes to assassinating the character of Mary Magdalene."

CHAPTER 8

The Disciple Jesus Loved

"There is one other puzzle we need to solve about the Last Supper."

"The Eucharist? You asked the Rabbi about the likelihood of Jews drinking wine representing blood."

"No, I know where that came from. It was introduced by Paul which he admits in *1 Corinthians 11:23* and only exists in the synoptic Gospels, which we have shown were edited by Paul's travelling companion Luke. No the real question for us to solve in the Last Supper is who is the beloved disciple, leaning on Jesus bosom, because if you remember his sister is the un-named person in Jericho?"

"It is always said to be John," I answered.

"Yes that is true, and if so it would make the un-named woman in Jericho, John's sister, a person who never figures anywhere else in the Gospel. But I have my doubts."

"Why?"

Holmes opened his Bible. "The reason it is said to be John is because of these last lines of John's Gospel.
'Then Peter, turning about, seeth the disciple whom Jesus loved following, which also leaned on his breast at supper. This is the disciple, which testifieth of these things, and wrote these things: and we know that his testimony is true.'
This is clearly saying that whoever wrote this Gospel is the 'beloved disciple'. So the answer should be John although some have even suggested it is a woman who he loved. But of course that cannot be so since John 19:25 states he is a man. *'When Jesus saw his mother there, and the disciple*

whom he loved standing nearby, he said to her, "Woman, here is your son".

"So the beloved disciple is clearly a man who is to take over being the son of Mary after Jesus death. Now John is a Galilean fisherman but the author knows Jerusalem well, as is evident from the place names throughout the book. He mentions, among others, the Sheep Gate Pool, Bethesda, the Siloam Pool and Jacob's Well. But what about Galilee? He hasn't got a clue about the area and the fishermen there. In John's first verse we read Phillip lives in Bethsaida, *the city of Andrew and Peter*. Yet Andrew and Peter are from Capernaum not Bethsaida. Then in John 12:21 we are told that Philip *was of Bethsaida of Galilee*. Yet Bethsaida is not in the province of Galilee! Is then the writer of John, a Galilean fisherman, or a man from Bethany, the suburbs of Jerusalem? The same man who Jesus is said to love? *'Now Jesus loved Martha and her sister and Lazarus.'* And later on in the same story: *"Come and see, Lord," they replied. Jesus wept. Then the Jews said, "See how he loved him!"* What do you think Watson, is it becoming obvious who the beloved disciple is?"

"You may have a point," I answered, "but I don't think you have conclusively proven it."

"Perhaps we can get the answer from Jesus himself."

"How on earth can you do that?" I exclaimed.

"Just listen to this from the Gospel," and Holmes opened a tab and read.

'Now a man named Lazarus was sick. He was from Bethany, the village of Mary and her sister Martha. So the sisters sent word to Jesus, "Lord, the one you love is sick."

"Let me repeat for you that last statement: *'so the sisters sent word to Jesus, "Lord, the one you love is sick.* Who is sick, Watson?"

I looked at Holmes questioningly and he answered his own question by reading it again.

"*'The one whom you love.'* And who could that be? You see Watson, no name or other clue of any sort is given. So tell us Jesus, in your own words, who is this sick person who you love?" Holmes looked down and read it out slowly.

"Then Jesus said to them plainly, Lazarus is dead."

"Why do people guess it is John, surely Jesus has just told us in his own words, it is Lazarus. Case solved! If there was an attempt to conceal Lazarus' name, it has not worked very well as it is plain as day that Lazarus is the beloved disciple and therefore possibly even the original writer of John's Gospel."

I considered it for a moment, "I must admit I am a little perturbed that all this passionate love is for a man, whoever he is."

"Roman times were different, our present obsession with sodomy makes everyone guard every word they mutter."

"At least we have recently replaced the death sentence with imprisonment."

"Ten years could be a death sentence for some. But there is one other thing about the term "the disciple Jesus loved.' It only appears in John's Gospel. But if we get back to the point of all this exertion, the missing Jericho manuscript."

"The missing Jericho Manuscript and the murder of Canon Alfred Lilly." I added.

"Yes indeed," agreed Holmes. "Do you remember what Lilly wrote that was missing from Mark's Gospel?

'And they came to Jericho, and the sister of the youth whom Jesus loved and his mother and Salome were there.'"

"My goodness! So the term 'the disciple Jesus loved' was also in Mark's Gospel."

"And this also tells us that this un-named, beloved disciple had a sister. And we know who his sister is, it is Mary Magdalene."

"Wait a minute. It could be Martha."

"Too true. But whichever it is, we obviously have an occupant of Bethany travelling from Jericho to Jerusalem with him?"

I considered this and realized, "That makes the passing of Bethany without stopping even more unlikely."

So we have either Mary or Martha and the other two women in Jericho, and it was felt absolutely necessary, for some reason, to cut out this particular story of them with Jesus."

"What on earth could it have been?"

"I don't know, and we still have no clue as to why all these crazy machinations around concealing Lazarus name in the synoptic Gospels and taking his name off John's Gospel. Surely if they put Lazarus name into the Synoptic Gospels and called John's Gospel, 'The Gospel of Lazarus' it would be fine. Or is there something more important we are missing?"

"The way you are going Holmes, if there is something missing, you will find it."

CHAPTER 9

Paris

The train from Calais to Paris was uneventful as was the flat landscape of Picardie. Holmes sat reading the Jewish Historian, Josephus who lived through the war with the Romans in 66 AD and was full of information about Israel at the time of Jesus. I started reading Tacitus' *'Annals'* and searching for the references Holmes asked me to search for. When night came we tried to sleep.

The temperature had risen quite a few degrees by morning as we pulled into Gare du Nord. I managed my own suitcase but we had trouble even getting Holmes case off the train. "This suitcase is going to kill us Holmes."

"Come unto me, all ye that labour and are heavy laden, and I will give you rest. Matthew 11:28," smiled Holmes.

Finally a porter arrived and loaded the case onto his trolley and wheeled it out of the station, across the road and all the way down Rue de Saint-Quentin to the Hotel Whistler, where we booked rooms.

Holmes was in his element as he spoke French fluently, I just about managed to follow what was being said but found it hard to speak and often slipped into Latin, which was part of my medical curriculum.

We dropped our bags and headed out to find 66 Rue Saint-Lazare, the address of Mohamed Elmeny that I had found from the shipping agents in Dover. The concierge told us to walk down to the corner, to Rue La Fayette and then a fifteen-minute walk to a right fork on to Rue Châteaudun that leads to Saint Lazare. La Fayette was busy with carriages of every kind, but I was becoming more and more anxious about confronting the murderer. Are we equipped for such a meeting? Holmes seemed to be oblivious to the danger.

We finally reached Saint Lazare and it was a street of impressive tall buildings with balconies. Would such tenements contain a murderer? Perhaps he lived in the small sixth floor rooftop apartments. But sixty-six was an opening into a courtyard and inside it looked like our man lived in the small porters apartment on the ground floor. Holmes knocked on the door while I held my breath and clenched my fists ready for a fight. The door opened by a portly man with a rugged face, dark hair and wearing a vest, nothing like the thin man we expected.

"Monsieur Elmeny?" asked Holmes.

"Oui," said the man.

Holmes and I looked at each other, was this our man and had Holmes got his description wrong?

"Mohamed Elmeny?" added Holmes.

"Non c'est mon frère, qu'a-t-il fait maintenant?"

I was able to follow this simple French, he had answered that he was the brother of Mohamed and then asked 'what has he done now', suggesting his brother was often in trouble. The conversation continued in French but I will give you the translation as best I can.

"Mohamed has done nothing," smiled Holmes to reassure the brother. "It is just that he has an old manuscript for sale and we would like to purchase it. Is he here?"

"No he was living here but then he has been travelling and since his return he has moved to live in Ménilmontant."

"My name is Watson," said Holmes, "and we are staying at the Whistler Hotel in Rue de Saint Quinten. He can contact us there, or do you have an address for him in Ménilmontant?"

"Wait a moment I will get it."

He went away, I gave Homes a questioning look as to why he was using my name, but he waved me down as the brother returned with a scrape of paper.

"The address," he said as he handed it over.

Holmes thanked him.

I could not resist asking. "Votre frère est-il mince ?"

"Oui il est très maigre. Pourquoi demandez vous?"

Holmes butted in. "Ce n'est rien, nous avions un pari. Au revoir."

Holmes pulled me away and we headed out of the courtyard and into the street.

"What the hell were you doing asking him if his brother is thin?"

"I wanted to know if you were right."

"But you made him suspicious. I hope he accepted my explanation that it was a bet."

"He accepted it and it is good to know that our man is a little less daunting than his brother if we are going to confront him."

Holmes shook his head.

"How about an early lunch, I'm famished?" I suggested

"Actually I do know a nice place nearby," said Holmes.

We turned a corner and came to a square with a majestic pillared building facing us.

"The Paris Opera," announced Holmes, "and there's the place for us. The Café de la Paix."

I had heard of the Café and I suspected the prices would be outrageous for such an impressive interior. And I was not disappointed.

CHAPTER 10

Saint Sulpice

After lunch we hailed a cab and headed for the Church of Saint Sulpice. Holmes had decided to go there first and locate the address of Mohamed Elmeny tomorrow morning. Paris, as always, was beautiful in the sunlight as we drove down towards the Seine passing the Louvre on our right.

"Watson we must pop in to the Louvre on our way back to see the sister painting of the 'Virgin on the Rocks'. Did you know there were two?"

"No I did not. But I am not going with you if this one is going to make you burst your sides again."

"I promise to behave. I was simply taken by surprise the last time. I am prepared to keep a straight face whatever jokes Leonardo has put in this copy. Actually there is no agreement as to which came first."

We crossed the Seine at the western point of the Île de la Cité on the Pont Neuf. The narrow streets on the other side finally opened into the square where the Church stood majestically.

As we walked up the stairs we could hear an organ powering regally through the chords of a fugue. Inside it was even more impressive, echoing round the second largest church interior in Paris. Holmes sat us at the back obviously to enjoy the recital. There seemed to be a group of some ten dignitaries seated together in the central pews of the nave. When the piece was over they stood up and applauded and there followed a presentation to the organist who descended full of smiles from the organ. We walked down the aisle and stood waiting for the congratulations to end. A priest approached and Holmes explained our purpose and he singled out the Bishop and brought him to us.

Holmes explained the tragedy that had brought us to Paris and Bishop Jules-Joseph Lebas called the others over.

"Messieurs, j'ai de mauvaises nouvelles, Canon Alfred Lilly a été assassiné à Londres." They all looked shocked. The Bishop introduced us, and some seemed to have heard of Holmes, and they fired questions at him about Lilly. Holmes gave them as much information as we knew.
"We have the address of the possible murderer, Mohamed Elmeny." Holmes took out the paper, "2 Rue Morand, Ménilmontant. We will interview him tomorrow."

"Be careful, it is a rather rough part of Paris," said the Bishop who then introduced the dignitaries, starting with the organist.

"This is our illustrious organist who has been reciting his new Symphony number 5 for Organ, Charles-Marie Widor."
We shook hands with each dignitary and managed to keep our surprise under control as some of the names were well known to us. A wonderful moustached middle aged, "Maurice Maeterlinck." And another equally impressive beard belonging to, "Stéphane Mallarmé." Then, "Claude Debussy."

Holmes was delighted. "I know your work well. I try to play your 'à l'après-midi d'un faune' on my violin, don't I Watson?"

"Yes he does and not that badly."

"But the violin cannot do justice," admitted Holmes, "to something so perfectly orchestrated for flute, clarinet and oboe."

"'Stéphane there," indicated Debussy, "wrote the poem à l'après-midi d'un faune.'"

We nodded our congratulations.

"Jules Doinel." We shook hands with another magnificent beard. And then we were about to be introduced to a fine looking woman when Holmes recognised her.

"Madam Calvé," exclaimed Holmes. "I saw your Carmen in London. Magnifique!"

"Emma also performed it at Windsor," added the Bishop. "And this is Émile Hoffet."

Sitting slightly apart were two monks in black cowls, they were oddly shaped, one very tall, the other quite short.

"These two Dominicans are visitors from Narbonne."

He pointed us all to the door leading to a room with food and wine laid out, but left the Dominicans in the church.

"Did you give Lilly the manuscript he was translating?" asked Holmes.

"No he did his translation on a document here," said the Bishop. "I don't think he took anything back to London from St. Sulpice."

"You do have a vast collection of manuscripts, I understand," said Holmes. "There is even rumours that you have the collection from the Compagnie du Saint-Sacrement."

The Bishop looked a little shocked. "You seem to be well versed in French history, Mr. Holmes."

"We know of the modernist movement but the Compagnie was such a secret organisation that I only know that it was later banned. I say this because I have been reading the Bible and now have a notebook full of contradictions."

"There are more than just contradictions," added Debussy enigmatically.

The Bishop gave him a frown. So Holmes pursued a different tract. "Why would a Mohammedan want a Christian document?"

The Bishop considered this. "If it was not for money then perhaps they want evidence for the Muslim belief that Jesus was not crucified but was substituted."

"Substituted?" asked Holmes.

"Yes it is sometimes said that it was Simon the Cyrene who was the substitute."

Holmes took out his notebook. "You know, I found that moment a little curious." Holmes read from his notes.
"This is from Mark 15:21. *'And they compel one Simon a Cyrenian, who passed by, coming out of the country, the father of Alexander and Rufus, to bear his cross.'*
"It says he was not a willing carrier, but they certainly know a lot about him; his name; where he comes from; the name of his two sons. It struck me as curious at the time. While I have my notes out, let me read you what Lilly was translating at the time. Perhaps you will recognise it." Holmes turned to the first page in his notebook and read.
'Mark 10.46. And they came to Jericho and the sister of the youth whom Jesus loved and his mother and Salome were there.'

"Now if you look at 10:46 none of these people are in Jericho and my research shows a clear attempted to hide or blacken several peoples names. Lazarus for one and Mary Magdalene."

The Bishop shook his head.

"Have you any way of knowing if a document like this is missing from Saint Sulpice?"

"Not really, there are so many. Do have a glass of wine."

We went over to the wine table. Debussy had overheard our conversation. "You need to talk to Emma about Mary Magdalene, she is the expert."

We looked round to Madam Calvé. "If you want to know about the Magdalene you need to make a trip to the Languedoc and her landing place in Notre Dame-de-la Mer."

"Landing place?" repeated Holmes. "You believe she came to France?"

"Undoubtedly," she replied confidently.

Debussy joined in. "Do you know about the Knights Templar?"

"I know of them," replied Holmes. "Nothing more."

"On initiation they had to perform two tasks, one was to spit on the cross." He waited to see our reaction. "And the other was that every new initiate had to swear on oath, *'Obedience to Bethany, the castle of Mary and Martha.'*"

"They swore allegiance to a building?" queried Holmes. Madam Calvé interrupted with another site to visit.

"I would also take a diversion to the little church of Magdalene in Rennes-le-Château near Carcassonne."

Holmes surprised me with his reply.

"We will do such a trip, as it seems key to understand what was in the missing document."

"And I presume you know of the prophesies of Nostradamus?" asked Debussy.

"Yes, I know of them but I have not read them. I am afraid I am a man of science and I don't believe much in prophesies."

"I am not talking about the prophesies," said Debussy, "but about the man."

"I would take Claude's advice," said Emma Calvé.

We came down the steps of Saint Sulpice with more questions than answers.

Holmes began, "That makes no sense."

"What doesn't make sense?" I asked.

"What possible reason could a band of warrior monks be swearing allegiance, not to Jesus, but to a building in Bethany belonging to people, who, if they existed at all, died over a thousand years earlier?"

"It does seem odd, but it does show a deferential reverence for the Bethany family."

"In stark contrast to the church's attitude towards them," added Holmes.

"Could that be why they were hounded out of existence?"

"Wait!" said Holmes as we reached the corner of the building. "Look at that."

Round to the right was a huge statue. Holmes approached, and it became obvious it was John the Baptist and the label confirmed it.

"What is he doing here?" said Holmes. "This is bigger than any other statue inside and that finger pointing is reminiscent of Leonardo's Burlington Cartoon. Remember in the National Gallery."

I shook my head, "I don't remember any finger pointing."

"I am not surprised. We will make that visit to the Louvre and perhaps there will be more finger pointing to observe.

CHAPTER 11

John the Baptist

We walked back to the river and crossed over to the Louvre. True to his word Holmes kept his laughter under control even though the same embarrassing rock formation existed. In fact the rock hand in the pool was even more obvious.

"Do you notice the differences?" asked Holmes.

"The cross is missing on the baby John and there are no halos."

"Yes but if you remember it said these were added later to the London version. Anything else?"

I thought for a moment. "Was the angel pointing in the London one? And the arum lily is missing."

"Yes Watson. And this one was painted first."

"How do you know that?" I asked.

"Leonardo was commissioned by the Confraternity of the Immaculate Conception, a group of monks elected to promote the Vatican's doctrine that Jesus mother was also born of a virgin. He offered this one but it was rejected."

"Why."

"It made the Baptist too important, placing him higher than Jesus and having the angel point him out. In the second one the pointing has gone. But Leonardo made the angels eyes look at John instead. The virgin's cloak is bluer, which is the convention for Mary the Mother. I don't know if they objected to the red cloak on the Angel as red is usually reserved for sinners like Mary Magdalene who is either red or green. Anyway he got away with the rock and the hole but he toned down the hand of God in the London version, but to compensate he added the arum Lilly with the erect stamen. There was still a degree of dissatisfaction so a cross was added later to John, and Jesus and the virgin received halos."

"That sounds reasonable."

"The real question is what episode is this picture representing? There is nothing in the Bible that says the Virgin is in a rocky cave with John and Jesus as babies, when an angel appears. Some have suggested it is the flight out to Egypt but where is father Joseph and of course the Baptist is not in that event.

"This lush scenery is hardly representing the Egyptian desert," I added.

"Very true," said Holmes

We puzzled for a moment but it was something neither of us could answer so we moved on and stopped where everyone gathers, around the Mona Lisa. From there Holmes went over to another Leonardo and stopped and smiled. "Who do you think this is?" he asked.

"I have no idea."

"This, would you believe, is a painting of John the Baptist. Remember the pointing finger, this is what the label says about the finger. *'The finger pointing to heaven, alludes to Christ's future destiny'.*

"Are they blind? With that knowing grin he is supposed to be thinking of Jesus' death and **resurrection**?"

"I must agree," I said, "it has nothing of the gravitas one would expect from a painting dealing with Christ's passion,"

"Leonardo is clearly trying to tell us something," Holmes added. "Remember the same single finger is on the statue outside Sulpice. I am certain this is not a pointing finger but a finger telling us who is number one."

"Number one? Are you suggesting Leonardo is saying the Baptist is more important than Jesus?"

60

"Not convinced? Then let us find the bookshop I want to show you something."

We went to the Louvre souvenirs shop and found an illustrated book of Leonardo paintings. Holmes flicked through the pages till he found what he was looking for. He turned it towards me.

"Remember the 'Burlington House Cartoon in London."

"Do you see?"

I looked, "What do you want me to see?"

"Watson! Come on, use your eyes."

"What?"

"I know the design appears perfect, but then hardly visible in the upper right?"

I looked again. "The pointing finger!" I exclaimed.

"Let's see what the description says.

'The Virgin Mary sits on the lap of her mother, Saint Anne. The Christ Child blesses his cousin Saint John the Baptist.'"

"What nonsense," said Holmes, "that older woman is not Mary's mother, Ann. The older woman has to be, Elizabeth the mother of John the Baptists who was said to be too old to have children. But the finger! No mention of the finger indicating what? In the blessing Jesus has two fingers but what number is the mother of John indicating but number one?"

"Why is it so faintly drawn?"

"Are you still having trouble with this, Watson?"

Holmes turned to another book and turned a painting towards me. "Look at his painting from the Sistine Chapel of the Last Supper."

"A disciple is thrusting the one finger up into Jesus' face. It is framed against black so it stands out. Do you think that *'the finger pointing to heaven, alludes to Christ's future destiny'*. Or is he pushing his finger into Jesus face to say you are not number one? And we know who number one is, don't we Watson?"

"John the Baptist?"

CHAPTER 12

The Arrest

That night we walked up to Montmartre. The stairs were numerous and tiring. Above us the dome of a basilica was taking shape. When finished it will tower over Paris. We arrived at Le Bon Bock Restaurant the walls of which were covered in paintings.

Holmes took a sip of his Sancerre and settled back with a contented grin. "Never have I been set such a series of fascinating puzzles by such celebrated company. Debussy tells me the Templars spit on the cross. The Bishop says the Muslims believe Jesus was substituted so never died on the cross. Madam Calvé insists Mary Magdalene came to France. How does all this mix in with our missing document and our discovery that the family in Bethany were persona no gratia to the early church."

"And Debussy said the Templars swore allegiance on initiation to the Castle of Mary and Martha." I added.

"Yes, their castle in Bethany again," said Holmes.

"There appears to be two sides," I considered. "Those who are for Bethany and the people who live there, and those who are against them."

"And did you notice when I said there were contradictions in the Bible, Debussy added that there were more than contradictions."

"What is more than contradictions?" I asked.

"Lies," announced Holmes.

We sat back and took another sip of wine as this sunk in.

"And on top of all this," added Holmes, "Leonardo Da Vinci announces in his paintings that John the Baptist is more important than Jesus."

"I wonder if this has anything to do with the Freemasons," I pondered. "They celebrate John the Baptist day as their most important day of the year?"

Holmes shook his head, "I have no idea. But I think I might be up much of the night with Josephus to see if he is able to throw any light on the subject."

"I wonder if anybody has ever gone through the Gospels with your attention to detail?"

"There are plenty of people who can recite verse after verse," said Holmes.

"But they are like parrots."

"Not so," said Holmes. "They are reciting Jesus' sayings, which are of value. I like 'let him that has not sinned throw the first stone' and 'the kingdom of God is within you,' which rather excludes the church's role. But of course many of these ideas were discussed by the Greek philosophers before Jesus."

"Really?"

"What I am investigating are day to day actions, which show signs of being tampered with, like the event in Jericho."

"That's what I mean, you have an eye that spots detail that others miss. Like that painting you found so funny. It has been with us for hundreds of years, in Paris and in London. It must have been seen by ten million, maybe a hundred million, but not one person in all that time has spotted the obvious rock and the hole. Surely that makes you one in a hundred million."

"How flattering. But that is exactly what I have trained myself to see. Those around us were irritated by my laughing: they were blinded by their own reverence."

"Yes, instead of being curious about your laughter they were disgusted by your lack of respect."

"I am sure Leonardo would like us to try to solve the puzzle than just to stand cap in hand...."

The starters promptly appeared before us, my Cheese Soufflé and Holmes's Coquilles St. Jacques. The soufflé was delicious and who could resist Holmes' scallop gratin in a wine and cream sauce topped with cheese and crispy crumbs. He devoured them and sat back with a contented grin. I chose the moment to ask Holmes if he really planned to travel south to Carcassonne.

"How can I ignore Emma Calvé, the greatest diva to tread the boards?"

"I'm not sure if I can afford such a journey."

"We will deal with that when the time comes."

"I think, Holmes you are getting diverted from the task set to us by my good friend, Adams. To find the murderer."

"And to locate the missing manuscript," added Holmes.

"But you are intent on discovering what is in the Jericho manuscript even before we have located it."

"Too true, Watson. It has certainly caught my imagination."

"But we may have the actual document in our hands tomorrow morning." I said.

"Yes it seems almost a shame to find the easy solution to my quest."

"Easy solution!" I exclaimed. "You want to confront a cut throat murderer without even the help of the Police."

"We obviously will not immediately accuse him of murder," said Holmes. "We will ask to trade."

This discussion as to whether to ask the police to join us on our visit to Ménilmontant continued through the main course and all the way back to the hotel and that night I found it hard to sleep.

At breakfast I had to insist Holmes involve the police.

"I usually have my pistol but here we are defenceless in the face of danger."

"Okay, okay, I give in," said Holmes finally. "We will get the police to join us."

We inquired as to the nearest police station, which was in the Rue St. Vincent de Paul, and then grabbed our coats and Holmes his brief case and headed out of the door of the Hotel for the police station.

Before we could adjust to the sunlight, six policemen and a Police carriage surrounded us. Handcuffs were snapped on to our wrists and two officers held us each roughly. A plain cloths detective spoke to Holmes.

"Watson?" he asked.

"Non," said Holmes.

He turned to me. "Watson?"

"Yes. Dr. John Watson."

"John Watson, je vous arrête pour le meurtre de Mohamed Elmeny"

"What? Me…. murder Elmeny? Holmes help."

"Il y a eu une erreur," pleaded Holmes.

"Passeports?"

"Passeports dans nos chambres."

The detective indicated for an officer to get our possessions, while Holmes did the best he could, but we were thrown into the carriage and whisked away. We had set out to find the police and they had set out to find us.

The police cell was rather dismal with concrete beds and the toilet a disgusting hole in the ground. We contemplated what had happened. Elmeny was dead and it appears the Police had got the information from the brother that, a man called Watson, who was staying at the Whistler was enquiring about his brothers whereabouts.

"Why did you give the brother my name instead of your own?" I asked Holmes as he sat on the prison bed.

"It is your own fault, you have made me something of a celebrity with your stories. So much so that he might have recognised the name."

"Now it is me who is to face the guillotine not you."

"Don't be so dramatic, Watson, once they wire Scotland Yard and they get the reply they will soon let us out. At least they have allowed me my Bible even though it was the Josephus I really wanted."

"They took you for a devout Christian."

We settled into prison life. Holmes reading and I bored stiff.

"Holmes." He looked up. "Why don't you spend the time, telling me about these contradictions you keep saying are in that Bible. At least it will relieve the boredom."

"Are you bored? I was quite enjoying the peace and quiet to concentrate." Holmes placed his Bible with all the tabs on his lap and turned to one.

"Okay, the first major contradiction happens right at the beginning of Jesus ministry when he finds his first disciples." Holmes read.

"'Mark 1:16 As Jesus walked beside the Sea of Galilee, he saw Simon and his brother Andrew casting a net into the lake, for they were fishermen. Jesus said, "Come, follow me,"
"And just like that they follow him. A lovely story we all marvel at and it is repeated in all the synoptic Gospels."

"Yes we all know that Peter is a Galilean fisherman," I agreed."

"Quite so," nodded Holmes

"Even the Pope wears the 'Fisherman's Ring' as part of his regalia. So what part of it is contradicted?" I asked.

"All of it."

"All of it!" I exclaimed.

"You may well be surprised. John's Gospel has a totally different story of the finding of these very same disciples, Andrew and Simon-Peter," Holmes turned to another tab.

"The next day John the Baptist saw Jesus and said to two disciples, "Look, the Lamb of God!"
When the two disciples heard him say this, they followed Jesus. Turning around, Jesus saw them following and asked, "What do you want?"
They said, "Rabbi, where are you staying?"
"Come," he replied, "and you will see."
So they went and saw where he was staying, and they spent that day with him. It was about four in the afternoon. Andrew, Simon Peter's brother, was one of the two who heard what John had said and who had followed Jesus. The first thing Andrew did was to find his brother Simon and tell him, "We have found the Messiah." And he brought him to Jesus.'"

"I've never heard that before," I gasped.

"No, nor I. Suddenly they are not the romantic fishermen, they are just followers of John the Baptist who spend time with Jesus before becoming his disciples. And the event is

not happening in Galilee but Judea, by the river Jordon not far from Jericho. Furthermore it says, Andrew immediately goes to find his brother Simon Peter who is living somewhere in Judea, not by the Sea of Galilee at all. But even more to the point, in 'Acts of the Apostles 10:39', Simon Peter is actually reported as saying:
'Now I, and those with me, can witness to everything he did throughout the countryside of Judea and in Jerusalem itself.'
So they are witnesses to everything He did in Judea but they are not witnesses to anything going on in Galilee."

I shook my head, "That's astonishing."

"Although John's version of recruiting the disciples is less remarkable, it does seem the more likely, so why do the synoptic Gospels move all this to the Sea of Galilee and make these same disciples, fishermen who leave their employ on a whim? In fact John's Gospel places most of the Jesus story in Jerusalem for example:
'It was winter, and Jesus was walking in the temple, in the colonnade of Solomon.'

"So Jesus is in and out of Jerusalem all the time not just at the end of his ministry

I had to admit, "It certainly appears to totally contradict the normal story."

"I even wonder if the name Jesus of Nazareth is part of this process of placing Jesus in Galilee. Nazareth was a very small village, so why was this insignificant appellation added to Jesus' name. Thomas of York makes sense, as York is a well-known town; or Alfred of Wessex after a known region, but Erik of Ecclesfield makes no sense whatsoever, as nobody but the people of Ecclesfield would have any idea what we are talking about. So Jesus of Nazareth is not only very unlikely, it is rather silly! Jesus of Sepphoris is more likely, after the major town three miles from Nazareth; or Jesus the Galilean after the region. Unfortunately, we already have the important rebel, Judas the Galilean functioning at the time so two Galileans at the same time would be strange."

"But what possible reason could there be for someone to try and place Jesus in Galilee as opposed to Judea?"

"I don't know, perhaps it is to remove the importance of Bethany, which is clearly his base. But there has to be something else. It clearly was extremely important to someone for all the machinations that I have shown."

Holmes turned the pages.

"There are two more contradictions associated with the arrest of Jesus. Firstly the synoptic Gospels have him arrested by a crowd with temple guards, but John has a different story.

So the Roman cohort and the commander and the officers of the Jews, arrested Jesus and bound him.

"A cohort is a battalion of around 800 soldiers and four centurions. In fact Josephus states that normally there is only one cohort guarding all of Jerusalem. So in John's Gospel the whole Roman Army has been turned out to capture this one peaceable man but in the synoptics there is not a soldier to be seen."

"That's very odd indeed."

"The other weird aspect of the arrest is that after his captured he is taken to the High Priest. In Luke this is High Priest Caiaphas but John's Gospel has a totally different name for him, High Priest, Annas. This contradiction becomes obvious if one follows Peter after the arrest. He tracks Jesus to the High Priest's Courtyard where there is a fire and as he warms himself he denies Jesus three times. In one Gospel it is the courtyard of High Priest Annas and in another it is a fire in the courtyard of High Priest Caiaphas."

"Which do you think is right?" I asked.

"I do have a theory but that is all at this point."

"Are you thinking that there are two different people," I suggested. "One who lives in Galilee and is arrested by Temple guards and is taken to one High Priest and the other who lives in Jerusalem and is arrested by Roman soldiers and taken to the other High Priest."

"No, that was not my theory but it is a very valid one for me to consider."

I must admit I was quite proud to get this acclaim for my theory from Holmes. But I soon realised how unlikely it was and he was probably just humouring me.

"Is that it?" I asked.

"Not quite. There is one more of a slightly different nature," said Holmes. "When Jesus is brought before the Jewish Council, the Sanhedrin. They find him guilty of blasphemy and sentence him to death. Stoning is the normal punishment for blasphemy. But then they don't stone him, they take him to Pilate who suggests: *'Take him and judge him by your own law.'* Pilate is quite right; he has nothing to do with the Jewish blasphemy laws. In fact as a Roman he would be worshipping a Pantheon of Gods so he would actually be a blasphemer in the eyes of a Jew. But look at the excuse the High Priest make in John 18:30: *"But we have no right to execute anyone.'* Are the Sanhedrin allowed to stone people or not? If there was such a rule it must have been introduced by the Romans so how come Pilate does not know about it? But worse still, straight after Jesus death in Acts of the Apostles the Sanhedrin stone Stephen to death."

"Do they really?" I asked. Holmes turned to a tab in Acts of the Apostles and read.

'When they had driven him out of the city, they began stoning him. They went on stoning Stephen as he called on the Lord and said, "Lord Jesus, receive my spirit!" Then falling on his knees, he fell asleep.'

"Doesn't Jesus save a prostitute from being stoned by announcing to the crowd, *"Let he who has not sinned throw the first stone,"* I added.

"And don't forget, the Jewish King, Herod Antipas, has just killed John the Baptists for questioning his legitimacy. So why take Jesus to a reluctant Pilate instead of to King Herod who would soon chop the head off, especially someone claiming he is the 'King of the Jews.' Something very strange is going on, because without this one statement in John's Gospel, the whole process of taking Jesus to Pontius Pilate makes no...."

The cell door opened and the detective entered with a smile. Clearly I was not going to have to face Madam guillotine.

"Please accept my apologies, Messieurs, Scotland Yard do confirm your story and Mr. Holmes they suggest I take you to the scene of the murder as they say you have a special skill of analysis."

CHAPTER 13

The Evidence

We journeyed in the police wagon to Ménilmontant. This was clearly the rough part of Paris that you would not want to visit at night. Mingled in with the locals and the ragged children was an Arab in a night sheet, an oriental shopkeeper and two Negros, all specimens from the various French colonies guarded by the famed Foreign Legion.

We pulled up in the Rue Morand and entered the guarded apartment. A squalid place with little furniture and no sign of occupancy other than a nightshirt on the unmade bed. The detective, Inspector Lebron, described exactly where the body had lain.

"Elmeny was here on the floor, blood round the wound at the back of his head. This bloodstained chair was on the floor. The murderer appeared to have broken this window to gain entry. Elmeny seems to have been packing to leave on a journey."

Holmes slowly moved from item to item. He studied the window; he got on his knees and studied the floor. He looked at the blood on the chair. He went into the bedroom where there were two suitcases, one open the other closed.

"From the footprints," began Holmes, "there were two attackers with very different size shoes. They did not break the window to get in as the broken glass is on the outside not the inside. The suitcases were not being packed for a journey they were being unpacked. The one unopened was the clothes taken from his brother's house where he had been living. The open one was the one he travelled to

London with and it is where the nightgown lying on the bed came from. It is also where the item that the robbers were looking for was housed. I suggest they simply knocked on the door to gain entrance. Elmeny was taken by surprise and they overpowered him and gagged and tied him to the chair. They located the object they wanted almost immediately. Then strangely they decided to untie Elmeny before leaving, not expecting him to put up a fight. They knew he had obtained the item they were taking illegally, so thought he would be very unlikely to go to the police. Unfortunately as soon as he was untied he made a grab for the object, and during the course of the fight he was thrown across the room backwards and his skull smashed the window. If you look at the corpse you should find a few splinters of glass in the wound."

Inspector Lebron was slightly open mouthed as Holmes finished and thanked my friend a great deal and offered us the Police coach to take us back to the hotel.

Once we were on our way Holmes made a confession.

"I am afraid I have not told Lebron everything."

"What else is there to tell?"

"The footprints of the two assailants had no separation between heel and sole. And the rope left a distinctive blood stain on the chair."

"What does that mean?"

"We met the murderers at Saint Sulpice," said Holmes, "and it was us who gave them the address."

I was shocked, "Who?"

The footprints were heel-less because they were made by sandals. And the cord was exactly the sort used to tie a monks cowl."

"Oh my God, the Dominicans!"

CHAPTER 14

The Opera

"They have left to go back to their Abbey in Narbonne," said Bishop Jules-Joseph Lebas. "They left rather suddenly this morning. Now I know why."

"What do you know about them?" asked Holmes.

"Very little. We assume Dominicans are visiting to spy more than any other task. They battle heresy as part of their apostolate. The order was founded by Dominic Guzman and appointed by Pope Gregory IX to carry out the Inquisition. And it was this Pope who authorised the Dominicans' use of torture."

"Torture does not seem to be a very Christian activity," said Holmes.

The Bishop nodded. "For the Dominicans torture was not regarded as a mode of punishment, but purely as a means of eliciting the truth."

"One can only wonder what truth is elicited by torture," said Holmes. "The truth that you want the victim to admit to. If he does not tell you what you want to hear, you torture him more till he confesses to what you want to hear."

"Too true, Mr. Holmes."

"The heretics were Christian, were they not?" asked Holmes.

"Yes they were Christians," replied the Bishop.

"So what was the difference in their beliefs to the orthodox Christians that they had to be tortured."

"Ah there were quite a few," replied the Bishop. "But the most frequent was that Jesus was not divine."

"Is there somewhere I can read of these beliefs?"

The Bishop laughed. "All books that held heretical beliefs were burnt."

"That's a shame," said Holmes.

"But if you read Eusebius' 'Ecclesiastical History' he gives a glimpse of the different heretical beliefs as he attacks them. Can you read French? I can let you have my copy."

"Yes I can, and that would be most useful if I am going to prepare myself to confront the Dominicans."

We followed the Bishop to his office and he obtained the book from his library and handed it to Holmes.

So what will you do now?" asked the Bishop.

"I wanted you to tell me," replied Holmes. "I did not want to go to the police till I gave you a chance to respond."

"You have to go to the police. There is no question as to allowing these murderers to escape."

"They are not murderers," interjected Holmes. "The crime, if there was one, would be manslaughter but even that is questionable."

"How so" asked the Bishop?

"Elmeny, a thief and a murderer," began Holmes, "is visited by men attempting to apprehend the criminal and recover the stolen goods. Elmeny puts up a fight and is accidently killed in the mêlée."

I considered Holmes explanation. "That could have been you and me, Holmes. That is why I insisted we go to the police."

"And you were probably right. But I don't think once we had recovered the stolen item, we would have untied Elmeny. We would have then called the police. But our

Dominicans were more worried about the Jericho manuscript being recovered by the police."

"Ah, I see." I said. "Of course it would become a police exhibit for everyone to see."

"And then returned to the rightful owner," added Holmes. "And that could be you, Bishop."

"Why yes, if it came from here. But did it?"

"Who knows?" replied Holmes.

"But now it is on its way to Narbonne," I said.

"It is interesting," considered Holmes, "that Elmeny did not let the Dominicans depart with the manuscript, but considered it important enough to put up a fight against the two of them."

"Perhaps he was paid a lot of money to recover it," I said.

"Or that he recognised something very important was in the Jericho manuscript," added Holmes.

"My friend has become quite obsessed with the contents," I told the Bishop.

"Yes I must admit it has opened up so many interesting questions. And none more than those posed by your guests yesterday."

"Would you like to meet up with some of them tonight? We are going to the opening of Richard Wagner's Opera, 'Parsifal' at the Paris Opera. I have spare tickets."

"It would be an honour."

That evening we donned our dinner suits, which we had recovered, with the rest of our belongings, from the police station and looking totally out of place we entered the Gare du Nord telegraph office.

"I must telegraph the Reverent to inform him that his friend Lilly is avenged and the murderer is dead. And to ask him if he would not mind adding more funds to pursue the missing Jericho manuscript."

I was slightly embarrassed since Holmes even put the address of our local bank, clearly giving Adams no real choice in the matter.

He then wrote out another telegram. "My brother might be able to help us."

"How do you think Mycroft can help?"

"He has a very good Jewish friend Ben Goldstone, he is Professor of Classics at University College. You may know the Goldstones who were friends of Disraeli."

"I can't say I do."

"We know what the Muslims think about the crucifixion and we know what the Christians think about it, but it struck me that the people who should really know are the Jews. It happened in their country and of course Jesus was a Jew. So perhaps Professor Goldstone can give us the Jewish perspective.

"I would imagine they think the same as the Christians." I said.

"Perhaps, but we shall see. Actually I must add another question," said Holmes as he wrote. "I need a little bit of Hebrew translation to see if we can clear up who the second Judas is at the Last Supper."

Holmes was obviously off on one of his theories and just wanted Mycroft to confirm what he already knew. That was his way in many cases.

Outside the station we took one of the many cabs and headed towards the Paris Opera House. The warm air and anticipation made the journey through the streets of Paris quite exhilarating. As we turned into Boulevard Haussmann we could see the Opera house ahead and we joined the continuous stream of hansoms and four wheelers that were rattling up and discharging their cargoes of shirt-fronted men and beshawled, bediamonded women. One felt like royalty ascending the steps. The interior was as imposing as the exterior and I was looking up at the impressive staircase and nearly bumped into Claude Debussy and Stéphane Mallarmé. They ushered us into the bar for a pre-performance glass of wine where we were introduced to several others. Some of the illustrious names I vaguely knew. Jean Moréas, Paul Verlaine and Charles Baudelaire. Holmes seemed to know them all.

"I understand you have translated Edgar Alan Poe in to French Monsieur Baudelaire."

"Merveilleux mystères pleins d'ambiance," replied Baudelaire.

They all entered into excited conversation. Holmes whispered to me. "You know we are surrounded by the premiere Symbolists. In fact I think Jean Moréas invented the term."

I was determined once I got back to London to investigate their work.

We were in our seats as the overture began. Debussy sat separately as he was to write a review and wanted to take notes without disturbing anyone. The music was solemn with ominous chords and fluttering violins as the curtain rose on to a magical forest of giant trees. Perhaps it was the location or the importance of our companions, but the Opera was the most extraordinary I have ever experienced. A strange story of the Templar Knights who guard the relics of the Holy Grail. Oddly to be worthy of this task a knight had to be celibate? Klingsor who is too wholesome to control his sexual lusts castrates himself to join the knights.

But Klingsor's mutilation does not make him worthy, and after he makes this dreadful sacrifice he is still barred and so becomes the evil one. He then injures the king Amfortas with his own Holy Spear, the same spear that pierced the side of the redeemer. Much is made of the pain the King is in and his desire for death. Only the 'innocent fool' can cure him and that is Parsifal. The scene changes from the majestic Grail Castle to the magical Klingsor Castle where spells are cast. The opera ends when Parsifal appears and declares only one weapon can heal the king: the same spear that inflicted the wound could now close it. He touches Amfortas' side with the Holy Spear, which both heals the wound and absolves him from sin, making Parsival the 'knowing fool.' Parsifal replaces Amfortas in his kingly office and orders the unveiling of the Grail. As the Grail glows ever brighter a white dove descends from the top of the dome and hovers over Parsifal's head. All the Knights praise the miracle of salvation and proclaim the redemption of the Redeemer.

As I left the Opera house and walked into the night I was completely spellbound and knew I would carry the experience for the rest of my life. In Le Fouquet's restaurant heated discussions began on the story, which I followed as best I could. Some saw it as magical others as bizarre and Paul Verlaine as ludicrous. Charles Baudelaire said it reminded him of the story of Abalard and Heloise.

Holmes enquired, "I don't know the story of Abelard and Heloise."

"It is a true affair that occurred around eleven hundred," said Baudelaire. "Abelard took Eloise as a lover but her father the bishop of Notre Dame attacked Abalard and like Klingsor in the opera, cut off his phallus. They are buried together not far from your exploits in Ménilmontant. The Pére Lachaise Cemetery. Well worth a visit while you are in Paris."

I could see from Holmes's face that we were bound for the cemetery first thing in the morning.

The discussions lasted into the night but whatever they thought of the story, all agreed the music was, *'incroyable et déconcertant et puissant et magnifique.'*

CHAPTER 15

Père Lachaise

We had a free day as we were taking the night train to Bordeaux, so we sent our luggage ahead to Gare d'Orsay. Holmes said he would take me for a walk along one of the hidden gems of Paris. We came out of the Hotel and headed left this time along the Rue La Fayette. The morning sun was not too hot and then at the end of La Fayette we turned right and before us was the Canal Saint-Martin. It was a most beautiful walk with tall trees on either side and big humpback stepping bridges over the water. After a while we crossed over on one of the bridges and stopped at the corner bar of the Hotel du Nord and seated ourselves at an outside table for a coffee and bread. Holmes said it was so idyllic he wondered why he lived in grey old Baker Street. After coffee we continued our walk along the canal till we turned left into Avenue de la République. At the end of the tree lined Avenue we came to the Père Lachaise Cemetery where we were charged to enter. But for our francs we were given a plan of the cemetery and a list of the best-known inhabitants. Holmes looked at the pamphlet.

"My God, everybody's here!" he exclaimed.

"Who is everybody?" I asked.

"The composer, Frédéric Chopin: the writer Balzac: the painter Delacroix 1798 to1863: George Bizet the composer of Carmen: the scandalous playwright Molière: the painter David 1748-1825 and not only Gioacchino Rossini but also

Beaumarchais who wrote the plays, the Barber of Seville and the Marriage of Figaro."

"Goodness me, that is quite a collection of illustrious cadavers."

"And they are just a few, there are more," said Holmes. "The map shows us where each - " He stopped in mid sentence turning quite pale. "Oscar Wilde.... he's dead?"

"He's here?" I asked.

"Yes. 30 November 1900. He died last year. I knew my friend came to live in Paris but I never saw reports of his death."

"It was reported in all ... wait you were in Italy at the time on the Count Messina affair. Remember?"

"November, Oh yes."

"If I knew that Wilde was your friend I would have told you on your return," I said.

"He called on me for a favour when he thought he was being blackmailed. He always sent me first night tickets from then on."

It was the first grave we went to and Holmes stopped for a while to pay homage. "I visited him a few years ago... it must have been 97 when he was moved round the corner to Pentonville Prison. He was not in good health then."

After a moment of recovery Holmes followed the map around the different celebrities reading snippets from the pamphlet.

"And here is the tomb of Abelard and Heloise and a little extract of their story. I will save that to read later."

We spent three hours among the dead, twisting and turning past glorious statues and magnificent mausoleums, none more so than where Abelard and Eloise lay at rest together.

We took a cab to Place de Bastille where we had lunch at the Petit Littre. While waiting for his Lyonnaise Salad, and I for my more substantial, Cassoulet, Holmes read the pamphlet to me.

"In twelfth century Paris, the intellectually gifted young Heloise, the niece of Fulbert, the Canon of Notre Dame, strove for knowledge. The only teacher in Paris that could provide the education that she sought was the famous philosopher, Peter Abelard, who was employed by the Canon to teach her. Though twenty years her senior, they soon found themselves so entwined that neither could resist the spiritual and physical desires of their bodies. Heloise becomes pregnant and the Canon in revenge, in a secret room in Abelard's house, cut off his penis. Abalard survived the attack and became an even more famous lecturer and philosopher."

"What an odd story to be so celebrated," I remarked.

"It is, but it relates to something in Matthew's Gospel.

"Really?"

"Now the question is, was this an attack, or was the story told to conceal the true nature of the event? Can the Canon on his own hold down this young man while he operates?"

"He could have overpowered him and tied him up." I said.

"True but why did it occur in a secret room? How did the Canon know he had a secret room?"

"What then are you saying is the real nature of the event," I asked. "And how does it relate to Matthew's Gospel?"

"I need my Bible to explain but are we talking about a ritual of some sort."

"A ritual! Cutting off the penis, a ritual?" I exclaimed.

At that moment my Cassoulet arrived and Holmes thought that, for the sake of our appetites, we should change the subject while we ate.

And the waiter added, "Bon appétit."

CHAPTER 16

Journey Through the Night

At Gare d'Orsay we picked up our luggage, or should I say I picked up my luggage but Holmes, since he had added another book to his collection, had to have a porter and trolley to lift his case on board. Holmes bought a newspaper, L'Echo de Paris, to see if the murder had been reported. We had a carriage to ourselves and Holmes sat down, took out his pipe and opened the paper.

"How goes the Boar War?" I asked.

"It doesn't look as if the French care too hoots about our South African adventure. They are still on about the Dreyfus affair and who forged what documents."

"Is the killing reported?"

Holmes turned a few pages. "Here it is," said Holmes.

"Do they mention us?" I asked.

"No the usual," said Holmes.

"The police claim all the credit." I said. "Not to worry when I tell the story the -"

"Look at this?" interrupted Holmes. "It's the review by Debussy of Parsifal." He settled back to read it.

"I think you must have something in common with Debussy because when you do your winding improvisations on the violin they sound a lot like a Debussy pre- "

"What!" exclaimed Holmes.

"What is it?"

"Look at what Debussy wrote in the review," Holmes translated out loud, "*'Perhaps it's to destroy that scandalous legend that Jesus Christ died on the cross.'*"

We were speechless, why had he made such a bold statement? Did he know something; did he have some special knowledge? Whatever it was the comment left us dazed in our seats. Not till the train left the suburbs of Paris did Holmes finally remember to light his pipe.

It was a long train ride to Bordeaux and I watched the pretty countryside of the Loire valley while it was still light. Holmes, filled the carriage with smoke and having finished Josephus' 'War' book, now sat reading his tattered piece of Josephus' 'Antiquities' book. Once the sun had set I tried to read Suetonius but was finding it difficult. I noticed Holmes suddenly making copious notes with long lists covering pages.

Slowly Holmes lifted his head and looked across at me. I say looked at me but it was more like he was looking through me. I looked back at him waiting. His eyes slowly refocused on my eyes and he asked. "Are you very religious Watson?"

I was a little taken by the abruptness of the question.

"Now my friend," I said, "have you forgotten you recommended that I read William Winword Reade's, 'The Martyrdom of Man'?"

Holmes seemed to have forgotten. "Did I?"

"Yes, when I was introduced to my wife when you were investigating the disappearance from the Langham of her father, Captain Morstan."

"So I did, I had forgotten."

"I read it and was converted by him to your beliefs."

"The book provoked enormous controversy didn't it," said Holmes.

"Yes, even Gladstone, denounced it."

"They called him an atheist," said Holmes, "but he was not, he had a presumptive belief in a Creator, but one ineffable and unapproachable, far beyond the grasp of the human intellect or the reach of petty human prayers."

"The book made a lasting impression on me. As you said it would."

"Then, like me, you are not attached to church doctrine," inquired Holmes.

"Have you ever seen me go to church, other than for weddings and funerals? I don't think church masses and rituals have much to do with Jesus."

"Good." Holmes then switched to ask, "In Suetonius, what are the dates for Tiberius' death."

Where was Holmes going with this question? I looked down at the book. "He lists dates in the old Roman way." I answered. "Wait a minute in the introduction by the translator, he gives us the dates of each Caesar." I opened the introduction where the dates of the Twelve Caesars were listed.

"Here it is." I said and read out the dates. "He came to power in September 14 AD and died 16th March 37 AD."

Holmes copied these dates into his lists and as he did so he spoke slowly to me. "I think Debussy is right."

"What?"

He looked back up to my face.

"I have been reading Josephus carefully and have come to the conclusion that Jesus was alive after Pilate left Judea in 36 AD and even after Tiberius died in 37 AD."

"But every academic places Jesus death in 32 AD," I complained.

"I would like to try and prove my point," said Holmes.

"You can try, but I cannot see how you can succeed because whatever you come up with I can trump you." I said confidently.

"We shall see," said Holmes and he opened his notes and began. "There appears to be a direct relationship between the death of Tiberius and the death of John the Baptist."

"Really?"

"It is a little convoluted but not that difficult."

The train sped through the night as Holmes began a long and complicated exploration. He said it was simple, but I assure you it was not that easy to follow, especially for someone who had had two glasses of wine, devoured a Cassoulet, a Mousse au Chocolat and a Cognac. I can only thank God for the coffee that completed the meal and kept me from dropping off during the explanation.

"You know, of course, the story of the death of John the Baptist?"

"Yes," I replied, "he was arrested by Herod for complaining about his marriage to Herodius who had been his brother's wife. And then Herodius' daughter, Salome does the dance of the seven veils and Herod offers her a prize and she asks for the head of John the Baptist. So they chop off his head and bring it to her on a platter."

"The story is much the same in Josephus," confirmed Holmes, "and in fact the name Salome does not come from the Bible but from Josephus. It would be interesting to know who invented the name of the famous dance as that is neither in Josephus or the Bible."

"The dance of the seven veils has always been part of the story."

"Yes it has, but it is not in the Bible or Josephus so someone, at some point, invented it."

"I wonder who," I queried.

"What is in Josephus but not in the Bible," added Holmes, "is that he describes the death of Philip in 34! And then he says Philip's wife married Herod. If this order is correct then the Baptist cannot complain about the marriage till after 34 AD, and Jesus is then supposed to function for two years after that, which has him still alive in 36 AD."

"Surely you cannot base your theory on a date Josephus may have got wrong."

"No I don't, because Josephus offers us more information. He tells us that to marry Philip's wife, Herod divorced his first wife, who was the daughter of King Aretas of Petra. Herod then married Herodias."

"Really, I've never heard of that divorce."

"It is the beginning of a chain of events because King Aretas' daughter went home crying to her father, who raised an army and attacked Israel. Herod sent his army into battle but they were completely wiped out. Distraught, Herod complained to the Emperor Tiberius, who sent a message to the legate of Syria, Vitellius, to either capture King Aretas and bring him to Rome or bring his head. Vitellius set out, but before he could attack, news came that Tiberius had died giving us an exact date of…?" Holmes left it to me.

"Of the 16th March 37 AD."

"And so Vitellius retreated to await instruction from the new Emperor."

"Caligula." I added.

"Caligula, yes. This is all impossible to fit into the Biblical timeline, which has Jesus preaching for two years after the Baptist's death and if the death was in 35 AD, this scenario has Jesus alive till at least 37 AD!"

"Perhaps it was just Josephus' bad structuring, or perhaps Philip divorced his wife while he was alive." I suggested.

"You are not alone in suggesting that," said Holmes. "But there is more evidence to consider. Just look how Josephus begins the second paragraph after he reports the destruction of Herod's army in late 36 or early 37 AD.

'Now some of the Jews thought that the destruction of Herod's army came from God as a just punishment of what Herod had done against John, who was called the Baptist. For Herod had killed this good man.'

"If the Baptist had been killed nine years before the destruction of Herod's army, surely nobody would link the two events. The destruction of the army in or around the beginning of 37 AD must have been no more than six months to a year after the Baptist's death, for them to be linked, which again places the Baptist death around 35 AD, three to four years after the supposed date of Jesus' crucifixion.

"I think I follow you." Although in fact I think he was losing me, but there was no stopping Holmes now.

"Also consider this: I have been quoting from my scrap of Josephus' *'Antiquity of the Jews'* book, which was written around the year 90 AD and describes the whole history of the Jews since Adam and Eve. But this first book, *'The Jewish War'* written around 75 AD covers just the hundred-year period that leads to the War which Josephus participated in. Now clearly the *'Antiquities'* book can only mention these events in passing but the *'War'* book will obviously cover them more fully. So if we turn to the *'War'* book," Holmes picked up the book and opened it, "and see what it says about the death of Philip, the divorce of Herod's first wife, the marriage to Herodias and the total destruction of Herod's army. What do you think we get?"

I was struggling to keep my eyes open but managed to slur an answer. "What do we get Holmes?"

Holmes slammed his hand on the open book, "NOTHING!"

I was startled to full wakefulness.

"Absolutely nothing. Not a word about any of it. No destruction of Herod's army, no John the Baptist and not even a mention of the important Legate of Syria, Vitellius in the whole book. Did he forget this most important person who sacked Pilate and played a major part in bringing a degree of peace to Israel."

"And whose son became Emperor" I added.

"Yes, and whose son became Emperor. Surely that is not credible nor is the absence of the total destruction of Herod's army, who must have policed Galilee for the Romans. If omission can be classed as evidence, we have the most telling evidence ever that these events had to be cut because they contradicted the Gospel story, by giving us a more detailed and telling account of the Baptist's death than the 'Antiquities' book does.

"You said this was easy to follow." I complained.

"You know Paul once bored a young man to death."

"How so?"

" It is here in Acts 20:9. *'Seated in a window was a young man named Eutychus, who was sinking into a deep sleep as Paul talked on and on. When he was sound asleep, he fell to the ground from the third story and was picked up dead. Paul went down, threw himself on the young man. "Don't be alarmed," he said. "He's alive!" Then he went upstairs again and broke bread.'"*

"Are you threatening to bore me to death?"

"I hope not as I have no powers to resurrect you."

"Then I will pin my eyes open."

"I have little to add just that I am pretty sure that John the Baptist was alive and kicking well past the supposed date of Jesus' crucifixion. And Jesus functioned for two years after John's death because He is reported in the Gospel as saying: *'From the days of John the Baptist until now, the kingdom of heaven has been subjected to violence.'* Clearly Jesus is talking about a person who has died some time before. So, if Jesus preached for a couple of years after the death of John, it would take us to around 38 AD, well after 36 the date Josephus says Pontius Pilate left Judea."

"While it is possible in principal," I smiled. "But as I told you I have a trump card."

"Let us hear your trump card then."

"No one will accept that Pontius Pilate was not involved in the death of Jesus because there is a clear statement in the Tacitus book you gave me, that Jesus was crucified by Pilate."

I took down my case and found Tacitus' *'Annals of Rome'* and read the relevant paragraph.

"*'Nero fastened the guilt and inflicted the most exquisite tortures on a class hated for their abominations, called Christians by the populace. Christus, from whom the name had its origin, suffered the extreme penalty during the reign of Tiberius at the hands of one of our procurators, Pontius Pilatus, and a most mischievous superstition, thus checked for the moment.'*

"Do you accept, Holmes that this is original material, and not a Christian forgery?"

"I do, as no Christian would describe their religion, as a *'mischievous superstition'* so I have to accept this is not a Christian forgery but what Tacitus actually wrote."

"Then you admit defeat."

"Not yet. I can see certain avenues where I think I can prove, that at the same time as accepting Tacitus statement as true I can show he does not actually contradict my timeline that shows Pilate had absolutely nothing to do with the death of Jesus."

I looked at him incredulously.

"A position, which I can see you think, is not only indefensible, but ludicrous."

"How can you accept Tacitus, who writes Jesus was crucified by Pilate," I complained, "and then say, Jesus was not crucified by Pilate? That is like saying black is white."

"I need to see an original Latin version of the text and then I will confront your very justified scepticism."

CHAPTER 17

The Languedoc

We arrived at Gare Saint Jean, in the morning. Bordeaux was certainly a lot warmer than Paris. After a few enquires we found a diligence bound for Carcassonne and settled in with the other passengers. Holmes had decided to split the journey by stopping to see the Magdalene church Madam Calvé had recommended. Émile Hoffet had given Holmes the name of a local priest in the nearby village of Rennes-le-bains, who he said spoke perfect English and would be helpful, not that Holmes needed any help with French.

The scenery slowly changed from flat vineyards, to rolling hills, to precipitous mountains. Finally we arrived at the magnificent castle at Carcassonne. We took a room at Hôtel du Pont Vieux and brushed off the dust of the journey. Holmes went straight out to the telegraph office to see if his brother had responded to his request. He came back with three pages from the telegraph office, smiling so I knew Mycroft had confirmed his theory.

"Three pages that must have cost a pretty penny." I said. "Or should I say a pretty franc or two."

"It did Watson, it did."

"So what did Mycroft get from his Jewish Professor?"

"That the Jews do not agree with the Muslims or the Christians, but have their own story." smiled Holmes.

"What do they think?"

"Well it is not what the Jews think, but it is what is written in their ancient documents. I suspect any modern

Jew does not want to have anything to do with the Crucifixion story as it blames their race for Jesus' death, which has caused them centuries of persecution."

"So what is in their ancient documents?" I asked.

"The Jewish Talmud states that Jesus was stoned to death?"

"What? I don't believe it."

"Let me read it to you: *'The Sages of the Synagogue, succeeding in capturing Jeschu, who was then led before the Great and Little Sanhedrin, by whom he was condemned to be stoned to death and his dead body was hung on a tree.'*"

"Why would Jews put the blame for Jesus death, fairly and squarely on their own shoulders?" I asked.

"This is not the only document supplied by Professor Goldstone, another, the 'Babylonian Sanhedrin' reads:

'On the eve of Passover Jesus, the Nazarene was hanged and a herald went forth before him forty days heralding, 'Jesus the Nazarene is going forth to be stoned because he practiced sorcery and instigated and seduced Israel to idolatry.'"

So we have the Moslems saying Jesus was substituted, we have the Christians saying he was crucified and now the Jews saying he was stoned to death."

"And we have Debussy saying it is all a lie, and not to forget the Templars spitting on the cross." I added.

"And once I prove my timeline is correct and it is not contradicted by Tacitus, then I will be advancing another proposition."

"You have accepted Tacitus statement that Jesus was crucified by Pilate, so I cannot see any way but the Christian way to be true."

"Don't underestimate me, Watson."

"Oh I won't. I have too often been caught out by your upturn of what appeared to be the facts. But I think you have met your match with Tacitus."

Holmes smiled. "We shall see."

And with that we retired to our rooms for Sigmund Freud's 'subconscious' to digest this new information.

In the mourning we sat in the sun having coffee in the hotel courtyard with the Castle rising overhead. Holmes was reading a five francs local history pamphlet about the castle and the local area. What surprised me was that a crusade was led against the Languedoc. One imagines crusades took place in the Middle East not here in France. The pamphlet said it was called the Albigensian Crusade, a campaign initiated by Pope Innocent III to eliminate Catharism, a version of Christianity that would not accept the authority of Rome. Figures of nearly a million victims were slaughtered. It resulted in the elimination of Catharism and the distinct regional culture of the Languedoc ended.

Holmes looked up, "I need to come to grips with the heresies, I am sure they must contain useful information if they were treated so brutally by the authorities."

"Information that undermined the Roman Church?" I asked.

Holmes shrugged. "Or undermined the story they told."

"Well you have already done enough of that, Holmes, for you to be tied to a stake and burnt to a cinder."

Holmes smiled, "I assure you I am simply following my nose, I have no idea where it all will lead."

We took a cab through the mountainous terrain till we finally reached Rennes-le-bains. We stopped at Le Therminus Hotel, and booked rooms. We dropped off our luggage and as we came down the stairs, on the landing was a painting of the crucifixion.

"I am beginning to identify people in paintings, thanks to you, Holmes. That must be the Magdalene bottom right with the red hair and green dress."

"And in blue is the mother," added Holmes. "But it is a rather darker blue than normal."

"It makes paintings more interesting if one knows who is who. Like, I see High Priest Caiaphas in the group by the cross."

"Or High Priest Annas. We have not yet decided which was the real High Priest," said Holmes as we carried on down the stairs.

We walked round to the church and found Abbé Henri Boudet in his Cassock trimming the plants in his little garden. A sinewy man with bright eyes that looked over his half moon glasses. He was overjoyed to see us, as he appeared desperate to try out his English. He talked nonstop over a cup of coffee and for the whole journey to Rennes-le-Château.

"Those are the thermal baths used by the Romans, we use the hot water further down at the Fontain des Amours."

"That ruin up on the hill is the Château de Blanchford. In 1209 it was conquered by Simon de Montford in the Albigensean Crusade. He gave it and the lands around to his comrade in arms, Pierre de Voisins. He was not popular."

The man seemed a mine of information and had a story for every ruin or strange geological feature.

"Down the road that way is Arques where the tomb stands that Poussin painted in his 1637 painting called, "Et in Arcadia ego."

"To your right, the ruin you see was the Château de Coustaussa, built in the 12th Century by the Viscounts of the Razès. It was the stronghold of the Cathars until Simon de Montfort conquered it. After that the Castle came into the possession of the de Montesquieu family. They were not liked."

It was not just landscape features; he was also able to relate some of those features to the stars.

"On the summer solstice from Le Bains, Venus rises directly in line with that crag, you could almost set your calendar to it."

The horse was beginning to tire, as the final twisting slope to Rennes-le-Château was steep.

"Renne comes from your English word as does much of the language of the Languedoc."

"I don't think we have the word Renne in the English language?" I said.

"Yes you do," answered the Abbé. "It is a bird."

"A wren," realized Holmes.

"Yes it is a phonetic similarity not a spelling one. Like oc at the end of Languedoc is your English oak. I have written a book on the subject, 'La Vraie Langue Celtique et le Cromleck de Rennes-les-Bains.'"

"What is a Cromleck?" asked Holmes.

"It is a Celtic word for a megalithic stone. We have a few here but not as impressive as your Stonehenge. I must give you a copy of my book when we get back."

I groaned at another book in Holmes suitcase, it will soon weigh as much as a Stonehenge lintel if he takes any more books on board.

The horse had had enough before we reached the top so we dismounted and walked the last hundred yards to the top and between a few houses to the little Church of the Magdalene. He called over the priest who was himself digging in his garden. I began to think priests here are more involved in saving the souls of their plants than the souls of their parishioners. After the introductions the two clerics entered into a busy conversation. Holmes asked if we could enter the church and they waved us in, as they were so preoccupied in their local politics that they were quite happy for us to look after ourselves.

We were about to enter when Holmes glanced at a Latin inscription over the door, 'Terribilis est locus iste.'

"I think I know what that means but you are our Latin expert Watson."

I read it "Terribilis est locus iste. I think it is, 'this place is... awesome' or 'This is a place of awe.'

As soon as we entered I noticed Holmes sniffed the air as if it smelt of awesome secrets for him to discover. Right beside us surprisingly was the figure of a devil holding and supporting the holy water vessel. Holmes smiled and the first thing that struck him when he looked up was a statue.

"What do you make of that Watson?"

"John the Baptist, baptising Jesus," I answered.

"Yes obviously, but did all those Leonardo paintings teach you nothing?"

"Well it does show Jesus being very deferential to the Baptist."

"It certainly does, but why is it here in a church to the Magdalene? And why was there an equally impressive statue of the Baptist outside Saint Sulpice? You can look at hundreds of pictures of Jesus being baptised by John and they nearly all show Jesus standing often taller than the Baptist. This church is obviously supporting Leonardo's personal view of John."

"You know Lilly was murdered on 24th June. Adams went to look for him because he had not attended the Masonic celebrations on that, the most important date in the Freemason's calendar, the feast day of John the Baptist

"So there is some link between these beliefs and the Masons who are considered by some to be an offshoot of the Templars," said Holmes.

"Why is John so important to them all?"

"I have no idea but I think this 'terribilis' place is going to offer us some interesting clues. Look there at the main stained glass window behind the altar.

"Yes it is wrong, as you said, Holmes, she should be behind him and they should not be sitting on chairs."

"Yes it is wrong on that count but remember there is in the Bible some confusion about who wipes Jesus feet with their hair. Luke says it is a sinner from the city, the church says it is Mary of Bethany, but this little church, dedicated to Mary Magdalene, is making it quite clear who they believe it is who did the anointing. No ifs or buts."

"Do you think they had permission to do these statues and windows or did they just do it off their own back?"

"I don't know," said Holmes but there is another feature of that window that seems to confirm one of my other suggestions."

"What's that?"

Look at Lazarus who is said to be reclining next to Jesus during the anointment. He is in exactly the same place and looking young and attractive as 'the disciple Jesus loved' is in all paintings of the Last Supper."

"So your idea that the anointment and the Last Supper took place at the same time, and occurred in Bethany seems to have some degree of confirmation here."

"And look at that window," said Holmes pointing to a smaller window to our left.

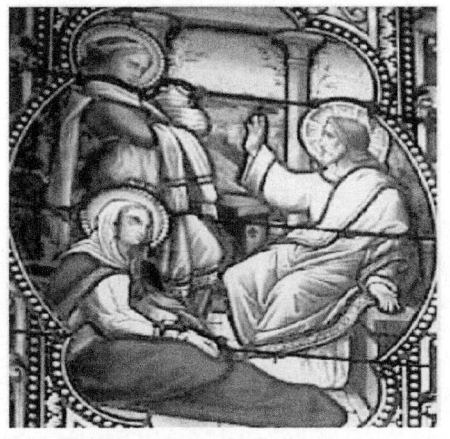

"That is the scene when Martha complains that Mary is not helping her," explained Holmes,"

"So clearly, Martha is the sister of Mary Magdalene," I added

"And, if I am not mistaken," said Holmes, "they are preparing the Seder."

"The Last Supper.'"

"And remember the Jericho manuscript stated that present in Jericho was *'the sister of the youth whom Jesus loved'* which is either Martha or Mary Magdalene."

I followed Holmes as he walked along the wall studying a series of more than ten bas reliefs of the stations of the cross.

"That's very odd," he said as he came to the end.

"What is?" I asked.

"Normally you would read them left to right but here they have been reversed, they start with this one," Holmes indicated the furthest left.

"And this one is rather odd," said Holmes as he stroked his chin. "It is night, and are they carrying Jesus in or out of the tomb?"

"It must be in," I said.

"And the spear wound is on the left but in all the paintings we have seen he is pierced on his right," Holmes remarked with his usual attention to every detail. "And above them all is a rose cross, which is the sign of the Rosicrucions who –" Holmes stopped in mid sentence.

"What is it?" I asked.

"Those two statues on either side of the altar."

There were two statues in pride position facing each other, of Joseph and Mary holding Jesus.

"I never thought I would ever see anything like that," said Holmes.

"Like what?" I asked, studying the statues carefully.

"It confirms something Goldstone told Mycroft."

"And these Madonna and child are a clue," I queried.

"Yes," said Holmes. "A big clue. I must see if our babbling Abbé has a substantial library down in Renne-le-bains."

We found the two clerics still deep in conversation outside a large unfinished house around the side of the church. Abbé Boudet noticed us. "It is interesting, no?"

"Yes indeed," said Holmes.

"François painted the altar image of Notre Dame in the cave."

"Notre Dame?" questioned Holmes.

The two clerics looked at each other strangely.

"I mean the Magdalene," said Boudet and changed the subject quickly. "Come and look at François' new rectory. I would like such a fine new building down in Le Bains."

"Very impressive," said Holmes.

"Villa Bethanie," said François, which rang a distinct bell for us.

Abbé Boudet pointed out over the landscape. "From here François can sip his wine and look over the whole world."

It was certainly an amazing sight to look out on.

"You see that distant mountain?" said Boudet. "It is the Pic de Bugarach and it is a mystery because the rocks on the top are older than those underlying them."

"An upside down mountain," said I.

"Henri goes out with his geological hammer tapping all the rocks," said François. "I suspect he is really trying to find gold."

"There is a gold mine down there but it was exhausted by the Romans," added this amazing mine of information.

CHAPTER 18

The Second Judas

Boudet had the screeching brake on the whole way down the hill.

"Where does your friend get the money to carry out such lavish alterations?" asked Holmes.

"François Bérenger Saunière has some important sponsors for his mission," replied Boudet."

"Like Emma Calvé," asked Holmes.

"I cannot say. He does not divulge their names."

As we came to the crossroads Holmes asked if we could divert down the road to Arques to see the tomb Poussin painted.

It was a stone sarcophagus just off to one side of the road.

"What is it doing here?"

"Nobody knows," said the cleric. "But I do have a copy of the Poussin painting, which shows that same mountain outcrop you see. And I have a copy of a famous letter that surrounds the mystery."

Back in Boudet's parlour he showed us the painting.
"The figures who are wearing Roman costume and two hold shepherds crooks," began Boudet, "they are clearly engaged in a riddle of some sort. Poussin gives us the impression that they have just stumbled upon the sarcophagus and are somewhat perplexed by its presence. They point, question the woman and contemplate. What they are pondering is the inscription on the tomb. The inscription on the stone

reads, 'Et in Arcadia ego', which translates as the phrase 'I, too, once lived in Arcadia.'"

"It could also be translated in the present tense as 'Even in Arcadia, I am here,'" I suggested.

Boudet thought about it for a moment. "The difference is, my translation suggests this dead person once lived in Arcadia, which is a mountainous area in Greece. While your translation might mean the idyllic place, which has become the modern meaning of arcadia, is how I once lived but even now I am dead."

"That is quite a difference," said Holmes.

"Well I say modern," continued Boudet. "But it was the Roman poet Virgil who gave us the new meaning in his work Eclogues, where he idealised the setting by inventing the image of lush vegetation, 'of cool springs, soft mead and grove' where shepherds roam singing love songs and untamed nymphs wander through the woods and rivers."

"In my mind," I said, "your village here has just that feel with its warm pools and trickling springs."

108

"What is the letter you say is associated with the painting?" asked Holmes.

Boudet fetched a book from his substantial shelves of books and picked out the page.

"This is a letter sent by Louis Fouquet to his brother Nicholas Fouquet after a meeting in Rome with Poussin.
'He and I discussed certain things, which I shall with ease be able to explain to you in detail – things which will give you, through Monsieur Poussin, advantages which even kings would have great pains to draw from him, and which, according to him, it is possible that nobody else will ever rediscover in the centuries to come.'
Fouquet was subsequently arrested and imprisoned being held strictly incommunicado for the rest of his life. Even the jailers were forbidden to talk to him. Some historians regard him as a possible candidate for the 'man in the iron mask'. Fouquet's correspondence was confiscated by King Louis XIV, who inspected them personally. The King went on to obtain Poussin's painting of 'Les Bergers d'Arcadia', which he kept secreted in his private apartments in Versailles."

"Is it still there?" I asked.

"No, during the Revolution it was removed and when the Louvre was converted from the palace to the Museum, it was moved there."

"Has anyone discovered what the monumental secret was?" asked Holmes.

"Not that I know of. But there have been many hints that there is a monumental secret of some sort. And fingers are pointed at the Templars, the Rosicrucians and even your church of Saint Sulpice."

Holmes looked over to me then back to our host and switched the conversation. "You showed knowledge of the stars and their positions in the night sky. Do you know of the procession of the equinoxes and could you explain it to Watson here?"

"Certainly. There is a wobble in the earth's axis, which causes the positions of the stars to change. So the rising sun appears to move from one star background to another every two thousand years. Ten thousand years ago the sun rose in the constellation of Leo, that is why some people believe that the Sphinx, which points to Leo, was built then. Eight thousand years ago it moved into the sign of Taurus, so the Bull became a sacred symbol for the ancient Egyptians. Two thousand years after that, the sun moved into Aries, the ram. At that time Alexander the Great conquered Egypt and was initiated into this knowledge by the priests at Memphis. Look I have a book with Greek coins where he portrayed himself on coins, with ram's horns as the chosen one of his age.

"Around the time of the birth of Christ, the sun was moving into the constellation of Pisces. As the chosen one of this new age, Christians equated Jesus with Pisces the fish and therefore used the fish as the symbol for him."

"I thought you would do a better job than I at explaining it to Watson. Would you have an image of the Zodiacal man in your collection?" asked Holmes.

Up he jumped and ran his fingers over the books. While his back was turned I sent a questioning look to Holmes. I had never heard this man of science be interested in astrology of all things. Boudet found the book he was looking for. He was obviously delighted to show off his knowledge and his library.

Holmes looked at the picture and then showed it to me. "You see different parts of the human body are associated with different star signs

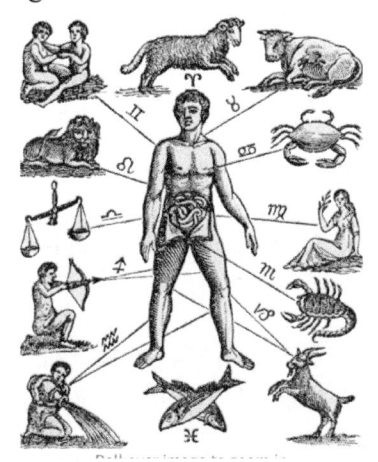

Do you remember the painting in the National Gallery of Jesus crowned with thorns by Bosch?"

"Yes," I said wondering where Holmes was going with all this.

"And you remember it was Aries who was putting the thorns on the head and Scorpio the hand reaching for the private parts. And see Watson, the two feet are linked to Pisces."

"Yes I see."

"Very good, then I think by breakfast I will be able to explain my theory about the statues up the hill. For now I think we should say thank you and goodnight to our wonderful guide."

We shook hands with the Abbé and made off to our beds where we would sleep and dream of Arcadia.

In the morning I was refreshed and ready to confront Holmes at breakfast. "Okay Holmes, what was last night's lesson in astrology for?"

Holmes took a sip of coffee, cleared his throat and smiled. "Do you remember that at the time of the birth of Jesus the sun was moving into the constelation of Pisces?"

"Yes."

"And what is the astrological sign for Pisces."

"A fish," I answered.

"A fish?" Holmes queried.

"Yes that is what Pisces means in Latin, a fish."

But Holmes was insistent. "A fish?" he asked again emphasising the A. "What part of the body represents Pisces?

"The feet." I answered.

"The two feet," added Holmes.

"Ah, I see. There are always two fish in the sign for Pisces."

"That's right and the only other sign that has a double image is Gemini which sits opposite Pisces in the Zodiacal circle."

"What is this Holmes," I said shaking my head. "I know you are not interested in Astrology and nor am I. Are you going to turn to reading tea leaves to solve your next case?"

"Let me get my Bible and I will put you out of your misery." He went back to his room and returned with his Bible that was beginning to look worse for wear for all the thumbing through he was doing.

"Remember I asked my brother to do a translation for me? Well there is a disciple called Thomas, sometimes called Thomas Didymus in the Bible. I knew didymus was Greek and it means twin. And Goldstone was able to translate Thomas from Hebrew. Do you know what the word Thomas means in Hebrew?"

"What?"

He looked at me and smiled. "It also means twin."

"Mr Twin, Twin?" I queried.

"How strange is that? Now as the sun moved into Pisces the two fish, there was an expectation of the birth of twins. Mycroft says this was very true of the Zoroastrian religion which was the dominant religion of the Persian Empire."

I was shocked, "Are you suggesting Jesus was a twin?"

"I have no idea," said Holmes. "but up that hill is a pair of statues, Mary with one baby Jesus and facing her across the aisle is Joseph with another baby."

I was speechless. However much I thought about it I just could not accept the idea was true even if there was a sculptor somewhere who believed it.

"There is absolutely no evidence that Jesus had a twin'" I pleaded.

"Circustantial evidence only," said Holmes.

"What circumstantial evidence?"

"Firstly Jesus has brothers and sisters as mentioned in Mark 6:3:

'Is not this the carpenter, the son of Mary, the brother of James, and Joses, and of Juda, and Simon? And are not his sisters here with us?'

"And if one of these is the twin it is Juda, who must be the second Judas at the Last Supper. So he was Judas Thomas, Judas the twin."

"That does not make him Jesus' twin. He could be anyone's twin." I protested.

"Certainly, said Holmes. "But the first moment Jesus appears after the crucifixion, there are two parallel verses in John 20, one without specifying Thomas presence and the next emphasizing it.

'Then the same day at evening, being the first day of the week, when the doors were shut where the disciples were assembled for fear of the Jews, came Jesus and stood in the midst, and saith unto them, Peace be unto you.'

"Now suppose critics complained that it was not the risen Jesus but his twin brother who was pretending to be the risen Jesus, so when John was added to the Bible they introduced this repetitive verse.

'But Thomas, one of the twelve, called Didymus, was not with them when Jesus came.

And after eight days again his disciples were within, and Thomas with them: then came Jesus, the doors being shut, and stood in the midst, and said, 'Peace be unto you.'

"There is no logical reason for the scene to be repeated word for word with Jesus just appearing to say again 'Peace be with you' except to add that Thomas was definitely present to counteract the critics."

"How do you know this was added and not there originally?" I asked.

"Because it says the door was locked for *'fear of the Jews.'* Now Jesus is a Jew, the disciples are all Jews so this has been inserted at a later date when Christians were trying to disassociate themselves from Jews."

I shook my head. "I just don't think I can accept the idea of Jesus having a twin on such flimsy evidence." I complained. "I can't imagine the three wise men looking in the manger and seeing two babies."

"You are right, I cannot say I believe it. But someone does. Mind you your example of the three wise men is a little unfortunate."

"Why?"

"While the two stories of the Nativity are very contradictory..."

"In what way?" I was not going to let Holmes get away with any unproven statement.

"Well in Matthew the birth takes place while Herod the Great was alive. Now Josephus places Herod's death in 4 BC. But Luke has the birth at the time of the census of Quirinius, which according to Josephus occurred ten years later in 6 AD. Furthermore Luke has Mary and Joseph living in Nazareth and go to Bethlehem for the census. While Matthew has them living in Bethlehem and only going to Nazareth after their trip to Egypt and...."

"Okay I accept there are contradictions in the nativity. So what is wrong with my comment about the three wise men?"

Holmes ignored my irritation and just carried on as if he were teaching a class of school children.

"Firstly there are not three," said Holmes. "We assume three because there are three presents."

"Gold frankincense and mir."

"And secondly they are not *'Wise Men'*, they are actually described as Magi. Now Magi are priests of the Zoroastrian religion. They were known to be wise and well versed in Astronomy so they knew about the sun moving into Pisces. Now in their religion there was an expectation of the birth of important twins. So if they followed that star information and came to a manger with twins in it they would instantly fall to their knees."

I sat for a moment. "Okay I used an unfortunate example, but I still cannot accept Jesus was a twin."

"Maybe you are right," said Holmes. "It is hard to accept but what we can say is someone out there does believe it and has acted on it by building those two statues and incorporating them into the church."

"Unless the sculptor did it and the Church did not realise the implications." I added.

"That's possible," said Holmes and sat back and sipped his coffee and took a bite from this mornings fresh bread. He seemed so happy.

"You know how I hate holidays," he said. "Sit around doing nothing, away from your books and chemistry set."

I knew very well that Holmes was lost if he did not have a case to investigate.

"If I need a holiday, a syringe of heroine will transport me as far as I want to go."

"I have told you often enough that is not good for the body." I remarked seriously.

"Yes, yes. But this journey is the best holiday I have ever had. There are puzzles presented at every turn yet there is no danger to ourselves."

"Unless we find the Jericho manuscript," I added.

"Yes, those who possess it have come to a sticky ending," he admitted. "But while we don't have it we can just play at solving these amazing puzzles set before us. It is like a giant crossword puzzle. 2 down – What happened in Jericho? 3 across – Who was the second Judas."

"5 down – Where is the Jericho manuscript?" I added.

"6 across -Who killed Jesus?" said Holmes.

"I have a horrible feeling you may upset a lot of people if you conclude something different from the accepted norm."

"What do I care of the accepted norm. I tackle problems for my pleasure not for any fame or fortune."

"I wish you would tackle one for a fortune because at the moment you are using the Reverend Adams money to undermine his basic beliefs. I don't count that as fair, Holmes"

Holmes shook his head, "You have me there, Watson." He knew he was doing wrong.

"I tell you what, Watson. When this is finished I will take a job that I have been refusing but is offering a lot of money, and with that I will pay back your friend so I can carry on guiltless."

"What job is that?" I asked.

"Leopold the second has been asking me to investigate the murder of the government official, Matrice Momumba, in his office in the Belgian Congo. You may have read about it."

"Yes I did."

"So I will sweat it out in the jungle, under the burning tropical sun to pay back every sous I owe your friend."

"Don't be so dramatic, Holmes. I know they will put you in a fine hotel with a big fan and you will solve the murder with one glance at the office."

Holmes laughed; he was in such good humour.

"When we conclude this adventure," said Holmes smiling, "and you decide to write it up for your journal, I think you should call this episode *'Holmes takes a Holiday.'*"

CHAPTER 19

The Expulsion of the Jews

Our Abbé Boudet insisted on driving us to Carcassonne, where we could get the diligence to Narbonne. But when he saw us dragging Holmes's suitcase out, he realised he needed another horse and went off and changed his carriage for the neighbours two horse version.

"I think we will be more comfortable in Pierre's carriage," he said.

"That we will," I said as we heaved Holmes' case on board.

"Pierre is our bee keeper, he supplies the honey for all the villages."

"I have often thought," said Holmes, "that I would like to retire to the country and keep bees."

"Come on Holmes, you are too excited by the chase to be involved in nurturing the humble bee."

"The bee is not humble," butted in the cleric. "Bees were the symbol of the Merovingian Kings. When they discovered the tomb of Childeric, the father of Clovis, they found the skeleton with his battleaxe, a crystal ball and more than three hundred little bees of the purest gold."

"Merovingian?" queried Holmes.

"Kings of the Franks till their line was ousted by the illegitimate Carolingians in the eighth century."

"Three hundred gold bees is quite a haul," I said as I joined Boudet on the drivers seat.

"Yes. And Napoleon knew that the bee had greater antiquity than the fleur-de-lis. So he decided that because the bee was the symbol of the rightful Merovingian kings, they would give him added legitimacy to rule as Emperor. Thus, when he was crowned, he made sure bees appeared prominently on his coronation robes." And with that the Abbé whipped the horses and away we went.

Boudet drove with considerable skill along the winding road, and again our 'mine of information' gave us a running commentary, from the majestic to the mundane, with scatterings of 'Bon Jour' to every passer-by whom he seemed to know personally.

"This is Alet-les-Bains which also has hot springs. In the sixteenth century the Huguenots burnt and destroyed the Abbey."

"That farm there is where the farmer, Marcel Leblanc murdered his wife, Celestine."

"Here in Limoux, during the French Revolution, demonstrators forced officials to seal the granaries, they demanded an end to dues and then ransacked the tax-collector's offices and threw records into the River Aud."

It carried on till the majestic turrets of Carcassonne could be seen over the treetops.

"There she is, the earliest ancestor of Nostradamus on his paternal side is Astruge of Carcassonne, who died about 1420."

"Nostradamus," said Holmes from the back. "Who told us to investigate Nostradamus?"

"It was Debussy," I remembered. "He said don't worry about the prophesies look at his history."

"That's right," said Holmes.

"I wonder what he meant by that?" I queried.

"Here we are gentlemen," interrupted Boudet. "The post office, the Diligence stop."

We thanked our friend, for all his help and Abbé Henri Boudet rode off a happy man.

"Damn," cursed Holmes." I forgot to ask him for his book on the Celtic language."

"Well that was a stroke of luck as we would have needed three horses to get here."

"Don't exaggerate, Watson."

"How old do you think he is?" I asked.

"He is sixty three," said Holmes.

"He's very sprightly for… Wait a minute, how can you tell a man's age from just looking at him?"

"And he was born in winter," added Holmes. "So he will be sixty four this year."

"Come on, that's impossible. How did you do it?"

"I saw his ordination document on his study wall," smiled Holmes. "It gave his birthday as 16th November 1837."

"Damn you Holmes! I thought you had some strange ability, that I would have loved to know."

"You see how mystification works," said Holmes. "If I had said his actual date of birth, first you would have known I had seen a document, but by just saying winter it threw you off the scent."

"You should go on stage Holmes, as a magic act."

"Mind you," said Holmes, "he needed to have been in his sixties to have assimilated all that knowledge and kept it in his brain."

"Perhaps he has a photographic memory, I have read in a medical journal that there is such a neurological condition. They can read a book and then tell you what is on every page."

"Talking about books," said Holmes. "We need to find a bookshop so I can get one on Nostradamus."

"Oh no," I groaned. "I thought we had just escaped another book."

Holmes dragged his case into the Post and asked about the diligence to Narbonne, which was not till two o'clock in the afternoon.

"I have, Watson, to deal with your scepticism about my timeline and I think Mycroft can help me."

"Mycroft might be smart but he cannot pull rabbits out of a hat to save your skin."

Holmes smiled and wrote out a telegram of four lines to his brother.

"Just four lines, Holmes, that is very frugal of you."

"It is not quantity but quality," said he.

We left our luggage at the Post and found a tourist bookshop in the actual Castle grounds and there were several books on Nostradamus. Holmes was going for the fattest but I convinced him to take the slimmest. We had two hours to kill before the diligence was leaving so we went back to our old Hotel courtyard where we had lunch. As we finished Holmes looked up. "Have you come across anything in your reading of the Roman historians that mentioned Christians or Jews in Rome?"

I smiled. "There is the mention in Tacitus, of Christians being persecuted in Rome after the Great Fire and the crucifixion of Jesus by Pilate."

"Alright, alright you might be laughing on the other side of your face after Mycroft replies."

"There is something else in Suetonius that mentions Jews," I said. "It states that Claudius expelled the Jews from Rome."

"That's interesting. The same event is mentioned in the Bible. What dates did Claudius rule?" asked Holmes.

"It was a short reign some ten years from 40 to 50 AD, something like that."

Holmes thought for a moment. "This must be a major event for the Jews."

"One would think so," I agreed.

"Then why is it in Suetonius and in the Bible but not in either of Josephus' books? It should be right in the middle of his 'War' book. Its not that Josephus does not mention Jews in Rome, he does, often very minor misdemeanours, but this is something huge, perhaps a riot by Jews or a major terrorist event to get all the Jews expelled from Rome."

"Are you suggesting it has been cut?" I asked.

Holmes was up on his feet.

"Let's get back to the Post and find the actual references."

We sat down on a bench in the Post and pulled out the relevant books' *The Twelve Caesars* and the *Bible*. I read my Suetonius reference first.

"Since the Jews constantly made disturbances at the instigation of Chrestus, he expelled them from Rome."

"By 'he' I presume he means Claudius?" asked Holmes.

"Yes we are in the middle of the section on Claudius," I replied. "So what does the Bible say?"

Holmes read from Acts of the Apostles: *'Paul found a certain Jew named Aquila, born in Pontus, lately come from Italy, with his wife Priscilla; (because that Claudius had commanded all Jews to depart from Rome:) and came unto them.'*

"Its obviously the same event," I said.

"Yes and very important, but not important enough to be in Josephus? Or...?"

"Or, they cut it out. If so why?" I asked.

"Why indeed," said Holmes. "I see another riddle for our crossword puzzle. 14 down – Who is Chrestos?"

"Obviously Christ," I said.

"Obviously not," replied Holmes emphatically.

"Why not?" I asked.

""Firstly the Bible reference does not say this expulsion was anything to do with Jesus. And secondly, what did you say was the tenure of Claudius?"

I looked it up. "AD 41 to 54."

"So you say this appears in the middle of his reign, say 48 AD."

"Yes, around that time." I replied.

"Now when Paul arrives in Rome some fifteen years later, in 62 AD, you get this at the end of Acts of the Apostles: *'Paul tried to persuade them about Jesus. Some were convinced by what he said, but others would not believe. They disagreed among themselves and began to leave.'*

"So even then they don't know much about Jesus so surely 47 AD is too early for Jesus' fame to have spread to Rome. Spread so much that many Jews were rebelling. And anyway why would Jewish followers of Jesus be rebelling? He is a man of -"

At that moment the diligence pulled up outside and we grabbed our cases and loaded them aboard. Or should I say, I grabbed my case, while Holmes dragged his till two strong men and the driver managed to lift it aboard.

On the journey Holmes made every effort to read his Josephus trying to locate a mention of somebody who could be called Chrestos.

"This is interesting: *'Now Judea was full of robbers who lighted on anyone to head them, he was crowned a king immediately in order to do mischief to the public.'* That rather suggests there might be several claimants."
He read on, his book bouncing in his hands.

Here's one called Simon who Josephus says was:
'so bold as to put a diadem on his head, and those around declared him to be King.'

"How the hell can you read like that?" I exclaimed. "You can read all that when we get to Narbonne. You are missing all this amazing countryside."

It did not matter to Holmes, he just kept turning pages.

"Another, Athronges again wore a diadem and Josephus says: *'this man retained his power a great while.'*

Finally Holmes stopped. "I think I am getting a bad headache."

"I'm not at all surprised," said I.

CHAPTER 20

Narbonne

It was getting late when we arrived at Narbonne and Holmes managed to find a porter for his suitcase. We followed porter and trolley round to the Hôtel Le Mosaïque and checked in. I had the Boeuf Bourguignon for dinner while Holmes had the Salmon en Papillote. With our coffee the waiter brought us a plate of small pastries.

"Qu'est-ce que c'est," asked Holmes.

"Navettes," said the Waiter.

Holmes was none the wiser as he meant what was in them, but when the Waiter saw his puzzled face he explained.

"Les navettes sont des biscuits marseillais en forme de bateau pour commémorer Marie-Madeleine et Marthe et leur voyage en Gaule."

He smiled and left us to wonder.

"Did I understand him correctly?" I asked. "These are shaped like a boat to commemorate the landing of Mary and Martha in Gaul?"

"That's exactly what he said," said Holmes.

"It was Madam Calvé who said that, wasn't it?" I asked.

"Yes, she said the Magdalene landed in Gaul at Notre Dame-de-la-Mer."

"Let's go and take our cognac in the lounge," said Holmes. "I will just pop up and get my pipe and my very expensive telegram from Mycroft, because he has done some brilliant research on this."

Once the Courvoisier had arrived and Holmes had his pipe alight and joining the other hotel guests in filling the lounge with smoke, he turned to the later pages of Mycroft's telegram.

"I told you Josephus describes two of the sons of Herod coming to live in this area after leaving Israel. So I asked Mycroft to see if it is likely that rich Jews would travel all the way to Gaul to escape the chaos in Israel rather than neighbouring Egypt and Syria. Mycroft certainly excelled himself on this one, listen to this:

'We have evidence that there was huge quantity of Jews in the area of the Narbonne by 600 AD as Archbishop Julian of Toledo described the region as 'a brothel of blaspheming Jews.'

Two hundred years later this same area called Septimania was given over to these Jews for helping the Frankish King, Pepin III to defeat the Moslems. So a Jewish Kingdom was established which crossed the border of France and Spain around Narbonne. We have clear evidence that this western migration was normal for the rich who could afford such a journey and we are talking about huge numbers as Jerusalem was flattened by the Romans. For example there is a book on Alchemy that Nicholas Flamel claims he found which states:
'On the first written leaf the following words were inscribed, "Abraham the Jew, Prince, Priest, Levite, Astrologer and

Philosopher, unto the tribe of the Jews who by the wrath of God, were dispersed amongst the Gauls."
These Jews were not uneducated peasants. An English monk, Theobald of Cambridge, wrote:
'The chief men and rabbis of the Jews who dwell in Spain assembled together at Narbonne, where the Royal Seed resides, and where they are held in the highest esteem.'

"That Mycroft is a genius," said Holmes shaking his head. "It is just a pity he is such a lazy so and so."

"He certainly gathered information from a wide variety of sources."

"That he did," said Holmes.

"But all those words must have cost a fortune."

"That it did," admitted Holmes. "But worth every franc because when you know that Josephus writes that the troubles started in the 40's, it means that this migration began not long after the death of Jesus. Could a rich Jewish family from Bethany have made this same journey to Gaul to join the Jewish community here? A community of well educated men including rabbi and even Royal Princes so these Jews like the Magdalene would know very well the story of Jesus."

"I hope that does not mean that you lean towards the Jewish story that Jesus was stoned to death?" I pleaded.

"I don't know yet. What I do know is that they are saying something that contradicts the Christian story because Mycroft said; Archbishop Julian of Toledo described Narbonne as *'a brothel of blaspheming Jews.'* Why are they blaspheming Jews as opposed to just ordinary Jews?"

CHAPTER 21

Tacitus

In the morning Holmes went straight out to the telegraph office and came back in good humour. He obviously had the telegram from Mycroft that was going to support his Crucifixion theory.

"Well?" I asked.

"Let's go to the Abbey and deal with the urgent business we are here for. We can play with theories later."

The Abbey was not a very large building and when we knocked on the wooden door it was opened by a fresh-faced novice. We asked to see the Abbot on important business and were shown in to a waiting room.

"Good morning gentlemen," said the red-faced cleric. "How can I help you?"

"Good morning Abbot," said Holmes.

"No I am not the Abbot, he is away. But perhaps I can still help?"

"Two of your Dominicans, Jaques and Nicolas were in Paris."

"Yes they were. At Saint Sulpice where they were sent to improve their education."

"We would like to talk to them."

"What about?" asked the Cleric.

"They have a manuscript that belonged to Canon Alfred Lilly who was murdered in London," said Holmes

"Jaques and Nicolas never travelled to London," said the Cleric.

"No, the murder was nothing to do with them," explained Holmes.

"Well I am glad to hear it, I was beginning to worry that you were accusing my two brothers of murder."

"No, no such thing," said Holmes. "But can we talk with them?"

"I am afraid not," said the Cleric.

"Why, we just want to ask a few questions," pleaded Holmes.

"I cannot give you permission, you will have to wait till the return of the Abbot," explained the Cleric.

"When will he be back?" asked Holmes.

"He has gone to Monastère de Prouilhe."

"Where is that?" asked Holmes.

"You do not know the Monastère de Prouilhe? It is the cradle of the Dominicans, where the first Dominican house, was founded by St. Dominique in the eleventh century."

"I did not know that," said Holmes shaking his head.

"It is just on the other side of Carcassonne," said the cleric."

"Carcassonne!" exclaimed Holmes. "We have just come all the way from Carcassonne."

"He will be back on Thursday," said the Cleric.

"But..."

And with that he wished us Good Day and left the room telling the novice to show us out. It felt like we were being ejected unceremoniously.

Once in the street outside we looked at each other.

"I have been kicked out of Public Houses less abruptly than that," said Holmes.

We smiled. "Okay I don't think we will make that journey back now, so we have three days," said Holmes, "and I suggest we go to Notre Dame-de-la-Mer."

I smiled, "If it is on the Mer then maybe we can buy costumes and go swimming."

To our surprise when we enquire about transport they said there was no such place as Notre Dame-de-la-Mer. We said it was where the Magdalene landed.

"Ah you mean Saints-Maries-de-la-Mer."

We were later to find out that the name had been changed. To get there it was best to take the coach to Béziers and then another to Saint-Maries, which is the Capital of the Camargue. We decided to check out of our hotel and to travel now to Béziers and continue the rest of the journey in the morning.

We, and Holmes's suitcase, were on the coach to Béziers by eleven o'clock and arrived in time for lunch at Le Boucan. Once the plates were cleared Holmes took out the telegram and asked me to get my copy of Tacitus.

"Right my friend," said Holmes. "I asked Mycroft to check an original version in Latin of the Tacitus statement in his book 15 of the Annals, and here it is.

'*Neronem noxae dedidit, et exquisitissimis tormentis exsecratus est genus flagitiorum, vulgus Christianos appellabat. Christus, a quo nomen ortum est, sub Tiberio apud procuratores nostros, Pontius Pilatus, et perniciosissima superstitio, in praesenti repressus est, extremam poenam passus est.*'

I read it and compared it to my Tacitus.

"But that is word for word what it says in my book," I protested.

I read it out to Holmes following with my finger the Latin at the same time.

"*Nero fastened the guilt and inflicted the most exquisite tortures on a class hated for their abominations, called*

Christians by the populace. Christus, from whom the name had its origin, suffered the extreme penalty during the reign of Tiberius at the hands of one of our procurators, Pontius Pilatus, and a most mischievous superstition, thus checked for the moment.'

"There you are, my friend," I smiled sarcastically. "Whatever you were trying to prove, I am afraid has backfired dramatically. Your theory that Pilate had nothing to do with the crucifixion of Jesus falls flat on its face."

"My dear friend," said Holmes with a smile. "I wanted to be absolutely sure the wording in the Latin was exactly the same as in your book, that is why I asked Mycroft to check it."

I was confused. "So they are the same. So there is now no question that Tacitus says Jesus was crucified by Pilate."

"Does he? Read it again," smiled Holmes.

"I read it again emphasising every word so there could be no twisting and turning by Holmes. *'Christus, from whom the name had its origin, suffered the extreme penalty during the reign of Tiberius at the hands of our procurators, Pontius Pilatus.'* Satisfied?

"Totally," said Holmes. "I am either deaf as a post or unable to understand the English language but I never heard you say the word 'Jesus' or the word 'crucifixion'."

"What!" I exclaimed.

"Did you say 'Jesus' and 'crucifixion', did I miss it somehow?"

"What are you talking about Holmes?" I complained, "It says Christus and the extreme penalty. Can there be any question Christus is Jesus and the extreme penalty is crucifixion."

"Christus is not Jesus' name," said Holmes.

"It is the name given to him?" I said.

"What does the word Christus mean?" asked Holmes.

"Messiah," said I.

"And the Messiah is a king who is going to lead Israel into battle and defeat their foes. Is that Jesus?"

"He was a different type of Messiah," I complained.

"Have you forgotten all those Messiahs I mentioned in the coach when I was looking for Chrestus. Remember Simon who Josephus says was: *'so bold as to put a diadem on his head, and those around declared him to be King.'* And Athronges who also wore a diadem. And these are not alone, Josephus says: *'Judea was full of robbers who were crowned a king immediately in order to do mischief to the public.'*"

I stuttered. "Are you really…"

"And I should add that the normal method of Capital punishment in Rome was beheading, which is therefore the *'extreme penalty.'*"

I shook my head in disbelief. "Come on Holmes, you are clutching at straws."

"Am I? Luckily my brilliant brother did pull a rabbit out of the hat and that rabbit trumps your quote."

"What in heavens name are you talking about?"

"Mycroft spotted something in the copy of Tacitus he saw in the British Museum Library. You see what he writes here: *I noticed that there was a slightly large gap between the 'r' and the 's' of the word Christians as if a fatter letter had been rubbed out and the smaller 'i' replaced it.'*

"Now Mycroft had no idea that we were searching for a Chrestus just the day before, so without any prompting he has spotted that c-h-r-i-s-t was originally c-h-r-?-s-t, suggesting that the person who suffered the extreme penalty at the hands of Pilate was not Christus but our famous Jewish rebel leader Chrestus who had caused all the Jews to be expelled from Rome."

I sat there for quite a while, saying nothing, just assimilating what had just happened. Against all the odds Holmes seems to have turned black into white. Even Holmes seemed a little shocked by Mycroft's addition to his argument.

"Is there anything else," asked the waiter bringing us back to the here and now.

Holmes shook his head no. "L'addition s'il vous plait."
The waiter went away.

"While you have your Tacitus there," said Holmes, "turn to the death of Tiberius."

I flipped through the pages.

"Now according to my theory Jesus died in 38 AD just after the death of Tiberius."

"Here is Tiberius death, it ends the chapter," I said.

"Turn the page," said Holmes, "and see if there is any hint in the next chapter about the death of Jesus."

I turned the page and must have turned white because Holmes looked at me and said, "What's the matter? You look like you have just seen a ghost."

I read very slowly to Holmes what was written in brackets at the start of the following chapter:

[The manuscript breaks off at the death of Tiberius, and Tacitus' description of the four years reign of the unbalanced Caligula is lost.]

CHAPTER 22

Béziers

Towering over the town of Béziers was the huge Cathédrale Saint-Nazaire. Our Hotel, Pont Nuef was at the base by the river. In the evening we dressed for dinner and sat beneath a tree by the cool of the river and ordered aperitifs. I had Calvados with ice that I think the waiter frowned on, while Holmes had the local Pastis de Marseille, which you mix with a drop of water. Holmes was glancing over a pamphlet he had picked up from the Hotel reception.

"It seems," said Holmes, "Béziers is most famous for a massacre by Crusaders against the Cathars." Holmes read the details. *"The first significant engagement of the war was on July 22 1209 when the town was attacked. The Catholic inhabitants of the city were granted freedom to leave unharmed, but most refused and stayed to fight alongside the Cathars. Abbot, Arnaud-Amaury, Abbot of Cîteaux, was said to have been asked how to tell the Cathars from the Catholics. His famous reply was "Caediteeos. Novitenim Dominus qui sunteius"*—*"Kill them all; God will recognize his own." Then followed the massacre. The doors of the church of St. Mary Magdalene were broken down and the refugees from the surrounding area around the town were dragged out and slaughtered'.*

I considered this. "The whole area seems to have been defined by the destruction of the Cathars."

"There are two interesting points about this opening salvo," said Holmes. "Firstly the date of the attack, the 22nd July which is in fact the feast day of Mary Magdalene."

"So the Magdalene church would be full," I suggested.

"Probably. And the second interesting point is the name of the church"

"Saint Mary Magdalene. What is so strange about that?" I asked.

"The Magdalene is not a saint. The Catholic Church has refused all requests to make her a Saint so far."

The sun was getting low as we wandered into the town and stopped to watch a group of men still noisily playing petanque in the failing light. It is a game similar to bowls but played on rough ground, so the steel balls are thrown in the air towards the jack. There was much merriment and I suspect gambling on the result.

"You see," said Holmes, "our game of bowls requires a perfectly flat lawn."

"Which is possible in our climate but not so easy elsewhere," I added.

"Think of all the games that the English have invented to be played on a flat lawn; croquet, lawn tennis as well as bowls."

"And cricket, although some of the pitches at Lord's have been anything but flat recently."

"Games are certainly a feature of English life," mused Holmes. "In fact remember how the Duke of Wellington claimed he beat the French at the battle Waterloo?"

"Yes, yes." I said enthusiastically. "He claimed he won the battle on the playing fields of Eton."

At that moment there was a big cheer and shaking of hands by our petanque players as the game finished abruptly. We carried on and found a pretty restaurant with outside tables, in a small square by a church with an impressive crucifixion statue outside.

Out of nowhere, Holmes suddenly asked me, "You must have treated some serious injuries when you were stationed in Afghanistan?"

"Yes I did," I answered.

"Have you amputated arms and legs?"

"Yes," I replied hesitantly. Holmes was clearly about to launch another broadside on accepted wisdom, and was arriving on my blind side.

"I presume, Dr. Watson, none of these patients died?"

"Not from amputating their limbs," I replied.

"Look at that statue," said Holmes pointing to the statue outside the church.

"Yes?"

"What do you think of the image?" asked Holmes.

"Quite impressive, the late sunlight brings out the bronze colour," I said.

"Yes, but tell me what is going to kill that man?" asked Holmes.

"Well..." I considered the question. "Um, I suppose exposure or possibly dehydration."

"How long would that take?" asked Holmes.

"A week or two, Jesus had been scourged beforehand after all."

"Forget it is Jesus we are just talking about a man," said Holmes and continued. "What about asphyxiation, he is hanging so raising the chest would be difficult."

"No, you don't generally breath using the intercostals," I corrected." "You breath using the diaphragm the muscles of which contract downwards. There was a prisoner we found in Afghanistan whose hands had been tied to a beam, but his feet were on the ground. He had been there three days and slept at night by just hanging on his arms."

"So we have a process that really does not kill you but is claimed to be the 'extreme penalty' and is so horrific that it is reserved as the capital punishment for slaves and rebels."

"You die of exposure," I complained.

"That is like saying the thumb screw is a method of capital punishment if you keep the prisoner in it so long that they starve to death."

"I don't think that is a fair analogy since Jesus was scourged first."

"Okay, scourged and then put in a thumbscrew," said Holmes smiling, but then became serious. "How can you have a method of capital punishment that does not kill you, and secondly how is that?" said Holmes pointing at the statue, "more horrific than having your head chopped off, which was the usual method of capital punishment. Which would you prefer?"

"Not a choice I would like to make," I answered.

Holmes continued. "I know which I would like. And to the Romans who went to see live humans being eaten by lions, that must look like a piece of cake," he said pointing again at the statue.

"Holmes you need to show a little respect" I pleaded.

"Very good," said Holmes apologetically. "Let me ask you something else. Look at the nails in the hands. Could you hang a ten stone man by nails in the hands?"

"Mmm… probably not, unless he was very thin. There is nothing to stop the nail tearing through. I would imagine the nails were in the wrists, between the radius and ulna. That would hold him up."

"I can't say I have ever seen an image of crucifixion with nails in the wrists.

"Maybe the painters got it wrong, like the chairs at the Last Supper. " I suggested.

"It is not only painters, there are cases of stigmata appearing and they are always in the hands. In fact in John's Gospel, Jesus is reported as saying, *'Put your finger here; see my hands.'*"

I shrugged.

Holmes summed up, "So we have a method of capital punishment that does not kill you. A method that is useless for fat people. A method that is supposed to be so horrific yet it is not as horrific as the normal process of execution. Can you imagine a statue of a decapitated man on the block being put in the town square?"

"Holmes, you are now being facetious. And this conversation is becoming a little distasteful just before we are about to dine."

Holmes took the point and ceased his investigation of the statue.

Being by the sea we had ordered seafood and at that moment the waiter appeared with an extra spoon for my

Bouillabaisse and a number of silver surgical implements for Holmes's spider crab. The food followed the implements, a ceramic bowl with my Bouillabaisse, enough for three of me, and Holmes's spider crab clearly looking ready for a fight. Round one saw Holmes bang with his hammer, crack with his pliers and gouge with his forceps. Shell went flying everywhere. Two pieces landed in my bowl, one fired across into the neighbouring ladies soup and a piece hit a passing waiter in the ear. By round three, the spider crab had to accept defeat and Holmes raised a fist in triumph. I applauded his victory.

"That crab certainly put up a good fight," I laughed.

"That he did, but I see the Bouillabaisse beat you."

"Pooh, I did the best I could but I am so full I am surprised it is not coming out of my ears."

We sat back with our Cognacs, as music started from a small café across the square. Guitar strumming, clapping and long held wavering vocal notes.

"That sounds more like Spanish music than French," I said.

"It is the passion of Flamenco, no doubt about it," replied Holmes.

I noticed Holmes was again looking at the statue across the square.

"Now what is it?" I asked.

"That man is flying," said Holmes.

"What do you mean?"

"The arms are not taking weight since they would be straight and the shoulders up. The legs are bent while the feet are pointing downwards so they would be unable to press on to the footrest. I would say that if the weight was being taking by the nails in the feet, then the body would be pushed away from the cross. I don't think I have ever seen a statue of a crucifixion that makes much sense."

"What is going on Holmes? Are you questioning the crucifixion now?"

"No, I do believe there was a crucifixion," replied Holmes. But possibly not the way you think of it."

"What does that mean?" I asked.

"It's just a theory at the moment. But there is more to that statue. Look at the cross?"

"Yes. What about it?"

"How long do you think it would take a carpenter to make a cross like that?" asked Holmes.

"You are asking the wrong man," I laughed. "I am totally useless at such practicalities."

"A tree has to be cut down. It has to be squared off otherwise you could not make a joint. You have to cut the joint and I presume glue it. Then I imagine you need to dig a hole of about four feet to stop it tipping over."

"Okay," I agreed. "Say for arguments sake it takes three days to make a cross. So?"

"Josephus writes that during a rebellion in Galilee in 2 BC the Romans searched the countryside catching bands of rebels and crucified them."

"So you now admit the Romans did crucify rebels." I declared.

"Two thousand of them?" stated Holmes.

"Two thousand?"

"Yes. Josephus said they crucified two thousand of them. Firstly, where did all the trees come from in Israel? Secondly did they have carpenters or did the soldiers carry tools. Thirdly how many soldiers were left to guard each group of rebels caught, to stop their relatives coming and taking them down, as you say they would be alive for two weeks. And lastly you allowed three days to make a cross, so we are talking about sixteen years to make two thousand."

"Well they would have had more than one carpenter." I argued.

"If they had thirty two that would still take half a year. And anyway we have talked before about the Spartacus revolt. If you remember Plutarch says there were six thousand rebels crucified on the Apian Way. Six thousand? What did they do cut down a forest to make six thousand crosses, dig six thousand holes and manufacture eighteen thousand nails? "

"So what is it you are trying to prove?" I asked. "You admit they crucify rebels, then you suggest they can't crucify them because the process is too time consuming. And then you add that it does not look right! So what is your answer to all this?"

"I have no idea," said Holmes shaking his head. "None whatsoever."

Holmes completely stumped, that must be a first. "Maybe you need to send another telegram to the brilliant Mycroft to come up with a solution."

"I might just do that," said Holmes.

"Mind you if you write a telegram with all your hundred points it will cost you an arm and a leg," I said smiling.

"And no doubt, Dr. Watson you will do the amputation."

CHAPTER 23

The Camargue

Next morning we followed the Hotel Porter's trolley with Holmes's suitcase down the tree lined avenue to the coach stop. After paying him off and buying our tickets we sat on a bench. Outside, across the road a group of some twenty people were standing on a temporary platform outside an impressive building. Then two horsemen waved people and carriages off the road. We stepped outside to see what was going on when a horseman with a spear came round the corner followed by a cow. What was all the fuss? Then following the cow came six enormous black bulls surrounded by four horsemen. The road almost shook to their tread and we backed back into office. They turned the bulls into the opposite building and the gates closed. The crowd followed into what turned out to be the Arènes de Béziers. We followed up the platform and in to the building. We were standing above the enclosure with the bulls below. One excited man turned to us.

"Il y a El Cortez."

There were a group of young men in white shirts and neat black waistcoats leaning on the barrier down below.

"Le torero?" asked Holmes.

"Le plus grand torero de toute la France. Vous voyez comment il regarde son taureau pour voir de quel côté il pourrait accrocher."

I did not quite follow and Holmes translated the last part.

"That bull fighter is studying his bull to give him an advantage when he faces him in the arena."

"I certainly would need some advantage if I dared to be in the arena with one of those beasts."

We were very surprised to find bullfighting in France and were very tempted to stay an extra day to watch the spectacle but duty called.

In the coach Holmes was again trying to read. Occupying one seat beside him were several of his books. The Bible, Nostradamus and the book and a half of Josephus. In his line of fire at the moment was Eusebius, which was adopted by his suitcase because it offered him some sort of clue about the different heretical movements. He stopped when we caught sight of the sea before heading inland again and came to a halt at Arles where several passengers were replaced by others. While we were stopped, Holmes took the chance to make some notes. He put down his Eusebius and opened the Bible.

"What have you discovered," I asked

"I am trying to make a profile of the missing man, Chrestus. I think I may have spotted a reference to him in the Bible. When Paul is arrested and brought for trial before the Governor he is accused... Let me read Acts 24 to you.

"We have found this man to be a troublemaker, stirring up riots among the Jews all over the world. He is a ringleader of the Nazarene sect.'

"Then Paul answers:

'They cannot prove to you the charges they are now making against me. However, I admit that I worship the God of our ancestors as a follower of the Way, which they call a sect.'

"So Paul says he belongs to a sect called *'The Way'* who obey the law, meaning the Jewish law, but he denies he belongs to the Jewish sect of *'troublemakers, stirring up riots among the Jews all over the world.'* The Nazarene sect! This strongly suggests that there is a Jewish *'troublemaking'* sect called the *'Nazarenes'* whereas Jesus sect is called *'The Way.'* Paul admits they *'both worship the God of our ancestors'*, but they are different sects. I am almost certain that the Nazarenes are Chrestus followers causing trouble all over the world, while Jesus followers are following *'The Way.'* The Way is the term Pythagoras used for his 'rules of life' and Josephus says the Essenes were close followers of Pythagoras. In fact much of Jesus' philosophy seems to have Essene roots, they are even said by Josephus to be healers as well as living a pure ascetic life."

"So you are building up a profile of Chrestus the way you usually build a profile of the killer in a murder case."

"Exactly that," said Holmes as the coach bumped back into life and Holmes tried to write but had to put down his notepad exasperated.

"Sorry," I said.

"Its alright, I will jot it down when we get to the hotel."

We were back on the main road when suddenly we turned right and travelled along a road that passed between flat grassy marshes, which looked like land recaptured from the sea. To our surprise, striding around in a shallow lake to our left were pink flamingos, something we assumed only lived in Africa. Further on in the distance, a rider herding some twenty white horses. Then on the horizon we could see the blue of the sea and in no time we entered the seaside town of Saints-Maries-de-la-Mer.

We checked in to the Hôtel Les Arcades and immediately after lunch headed for the dominating building that appeared to be a fortress but was in fact the church. Oddly next to it was a fairground and toyshops with hundreds of little figurines on every subject from local peasants to

Kings, clerics, gypsy horsemen, to Biblical characters. There was a small bookshop, which should give us the information we were looking for. When we entered we were welcomed with a smile from an attractive lady in her late thirties but with a trim figure and neat dress.

"Bonjour messieurs, or should I say good afternoon Gentlemen, I am afraid I have no English books."

"How do you know we are English?" I asked.

"There are certain details in your dress that tells me you are English. You are certainly more use to cloud than sun."

"That's very clever, isn't it Holmes?"

He was watching the lady curiously. She spoke English with a lovely French accent.

"Yes, and you are not tourists I see, but seekers after knowledge."

"Now how could you know that?" I asked.

"I watched you walk straight past the tourist shops and directly here."

"Well Holmes what do you say to that?"

"You are very observant Mademoiselle," began Holmes. "I say Mademoiselle because you are not married but you do have a cat, which is not alone as your invalid mother is at home. And may I say you speak English very well for someone who learnt it from reading English books."

"Sir," she said. "You would make a good detective, as you spotted I have no ring and there are cat hairs on my cardigan. But how do you know I learnt English from reading books?"

You pronounce certain words as written not how we actually say them."

"How's that Holmes, I thought her English perfect?"

"Mademoiselle said 'clood' for the word spelt C-L-O-U-D, where we actually pronounce it as C-L-A-W-D.

"I see I need to speak more and read less," said she. "But how do you know I have an invalid mother?"

Holmes smiled enigmatically, "You must not remove all my air of mystery or I will become too boring."

We all burst out laughing at the exchange. Our Mademoiselle slipped on her spectacles to return to an efficient sales lady. "Now gentlemen what are you looking for?"

"Just a book on the story of the Magdalene," said Holmes, "and her supposed landing here."

"A small one," I added.

"There is no doubt, Sir, that she landed here. There is a painting on the wall behind you of the event. It is the Queen of Marseilles welcoming the Magdalene."

"A painting does not make it true," said Holmes. "Nor the Navettes that we tasted in the shape of a boat."

"You tried them," said she. "Very good are they not?"

"Very good," I agreed.

"Yes, said Holmes, "he ate four."

"Now," she said. "I have many books on the subject but they are all in French."

"Ce n'est pas un problème," said Holmes, "je peux lire parfaitement en français."

"Ah, très bien," she smiled. "So here are a number of books on the subject."

""Do you know the Magdalene story well?" I asked.

"Very well," she replied.

"Then instead of a book perhaps you could join us for dinner and tell us," I asked hopefully. "Sir, there, has a case load of books and another one will split the seams of his suitcase. You are obviously well versed in the subject, so if we can get the story direct from you it would help."

"Well..."

"Let me introduce myself, I am Dr. John Watson, and my friend is Mr. Sherlock Holmes."

"Vous plaisantez!" she exclaimed.

"What is it?" I asked.

"I am not a fool," she complained. "I have read two of the books, I know who Sherlock Holmes is. A fictional detective in stories."

"No, which books did you read?" I asked.

"One about a boy kidnapped from school and another about a lady on a bicycle."

"Ah they are later ones, by the time I wrote those accounts everybody in England knew Holmes was a real person so I did not have to explain."

She looked at me and shook her head.

"Holmes, help me." I pleaded.

"Perhaps, Mademoiselle I can put your mind at rest." Holmes felt into his inside pocket and pulled out his passport and opened the picture page and turned it to her.

"Ah yes," I agreed, "and I can get my passport from the hotel."

She put her hand to her head trying to readjust her beliefs. "Oh, I am so sorry. I...."

"No," said Holmes. "I am quite flattered to think I am a fictional character."

"So will you have dinner with us, Ma...., what is your name, Mademoiselle?" I asked.

"Perrine Marcel."

"Say yes, Perrine," added Holmes.

"We are staying at the Hôtel Les Arcades." I added. "If you think that is a suitable place or perhaps you could recommend somewhere."

She smiled, "On the other side of the church in Place d'Église, there is La Bohème which is not too formal," Perrine suggested.

"So you will join us?" I asked hopefully.

"If you don't mind the odd cat hair on my dress."

We laughed and arranged to eat at eight.

Holmes taunted me all the way back to the Hotel.

"I have never known you to be so forward, Watson."

"I will do anything to save us from carrying another book. And you were never going to ask her," I teased, "I could see you liked her."

"You know very well I am a confirmed bachelor."

"She was very bright though," I added.

"Yes," said Holmes. "And had a good sense of humour."

"Ahhh I smell a holiday romance for my 'Holmes takes a Holiday' episode."

CHAPTER 24

Mary Magdalene

We had champagne as an aperitif, which is not uncommon in France, and we chatted about many things with Perrine. We told her about the bulls we had seen and she explained how they were bred here on the Camargue by the Gitan.

I was confused but Holmes explained.

"Gitan is not the cigarette, Watson. Gitan is gypsy; Gitanes is the cigarette."

"And Gitanes is a female gypsy," added Perrine. "There are many in these parts, they speak Spanish and you can here some of the best Flamenco sung here in their bars."

"That explains the bullfighting and the music we heard the other day," said Holmes.

"You can see a bullfight at the Roman Amphitheatre in Nimes, it is quite a spectacle," said Perrine. "But I do not like those where the bull dies. Here in our bullring we do not kill the bulls, rosettes are placed between the horns and our young men leap over the horns athletically to retrieve the prize."

"That may be the most original," said Holmes, "since I have seen images in Crete from the ancient Minoan civilization, of men leaping bulls as a sport."

"I think the Minoans were around 2000 BC, if I am not mistaken," I added.

"Even earlier," said Holmes, "but they were destroyed by the Thera volcanic explosion around 1500 BC."

The conversation then turned to our quest for the Jericho Manuscript.

"It appears that it was a copy of a missing section of Marks Gospel," I said.

Holmes continued, "It was Mark 10:46, which continued, *'And they came to Jericho and the sister of the youth whom Jesus loved and his mother and Salome were there...'*
"We believe Lazarus is the disciple Jesus loved, continued Holmes, "and so that makes his sister, Mary Magdalene or Martha."

"Interesting," said Perrine. "A Salome figures with Mary Magdalene and Martha in our story here. But here comes the waiter with your steaks so I will continue after we have eaten."

Both of us had ordered steaks since they had been highly recommended by Perrine as the bulls were bred locally and they certainly proved to be tender and full of flavour and they soon disappeared from our plates. We sat back with our Cognacs to listen to Perrine's story, which began with the death of Jesus.

It appears that being persecuted a group including the Magdalene travelled to Alexandria and then crossed the sea heading for Marseilles. Accounts vary, but legend says that along with Mary Magdalene were Mary Salomé, Mary Jacobé, Martha, Lazarus and Maximin, who was one of the seventy-two mentioned in Acts. Also with them was their Egyptian servant Sara."

We had earlier visited the church and seen the statue of the boat with the Maries in it.

"After a rough passage at sea," she continued, "They were blown off course and landed here at Sainte Maries. Strangely there is very little celebration from the church but the town is a pilgrimage site for the gypsies, who come to worship their patron, the Egyptian servant, known as 'Black Sara' for her dark skin. There is a huge procession every year when an icon of the blessed saint is carried into the sea, accompanied by thousands of fervent followers."

It appears from Perrine's account that after landing the men headed east, where Lazarus became the first bishop of Marseille and Maximin became the first bishop of Aix-en-Provence. Martha went north, towards Avignon and ended up in Tarascon where she lived and died and is buried there in St. Martha's Church. As for Mary Magdalene, she joined Lazarus and helped him convert the people of Marseille to Christianity. Then she continued on, to the mountains further east, where she settled in a lonely grotto called now, La Sainte Baume, in contemplation and prayer. After many years in her grotto, Mary Magdalene felt that her end was near, so she made her way to Aix-en-Provence to her old friend Maximin. She died there in his arms soon after and some of her remains are said to reside in the Basilica of Mary Magdalene in the town of Saint-Maximin-la-Sainte-Baume.

Holmes considered the information. "For legend it seems very specific. But there is one thing I don't think is true."

"What's that?" asked Perrine.

"Mary Magdalene was a Jewess. At this early date there were no Christians. Paul who seemed to separate the religions was still in prison in Israel. Jesus' brother James who was called Bishop of Bishops was a Jew for all his life, till he died in 62 AD. So Mary Magdalene was not converting the Jews of the area to Christianity but to 'The Way' a Jewish faction similar to Essene philosophy that appears to be the beliefs of Jesus. And I would suggest she died a Jewess."

"That is an interesting observation," said Perrine.

"Remember the painting the Priest did himself on the altar of the church of Rennes-le-Château?" I said. "It was Magdalene in the cave."

"You can visit the cave," said Perrine. "It is now managed by the Dominican order."

"Oh no," I moaned. "The way we were kicked out of their Abbey suggests we might be personas non grata."

Perrine smiled, "I am sure they will let you in. But be sure to take sturdy shoes because it is a forty minute walk to get there."

"I better rest up then," I yawned, "I will head back to the Hotel as I am feeling a little tired" And with that I beat a hasty retreat and left Holmes and Perrine chatting at the table in La Bohème.

CHAPTER 25

Nostradamus

The next morning we woke late, had our bread and coffee, bought swimming costumes and headed for the beach. The sand was warm and the sea a pleasant temperature. I jumped the waves while Holmes headed out past the waves and swam around like an Olympic athlete.

I shouted to him. "Beats the stony beach at Brighton and those cold grey waters."

He nodded between strokes. Watching him I thought this really is 'Holmes takes a Holiday.' What I would give to have a camera to take a holiday snap of Holmes on the beach in his swimsuit, but as I turned a wave hit me in the face and I got a mouthful of salty water. When I opened my eyes there was Holmes beside me with arms raised and leaping like a salmon and shouting, "Nostradamus! Nostradamus!"

"What is it?"

"What a buffoon I am," he shouted, "What a blind fool."

"What?"

"Nostradamus," he repeated.

"Yes I got that, what about him?"

"Nostradamus is Latin for Notre Dame!"

And with that he leaped out of the water, and rushed across the sand and headed back to the Hotel half naked.

That was the closest thing I had ever seen to Archimedes, jumping out of his bath shouting Eureka!

When I got back I half expected Holmes to still be in his wet costume, but he had at least taken the time to dry himself and get dressed before he attacked the book on Nostradamus, which we had bought in Carcassonne Castle. He was sitting in the hotel restaurant reading.

"Well what did he prophesy that made you leap out of the water like a flying fish?"

"Remember what Debussy said, it is not the prophesies but his life."

"What about his life?"

"Listen to this," said Holmes and he read from the book: "*He was born on 14th December 1503 in Saint-Rémy-de-Provence. The earliest ancestor who can be identified on the paternal side is Astruge of Carcassonne who died about 1420.*"

"The Abeé; our 'mine of information' said exactly that."

"Yes, that's right," said Holmes and he read on. "*He was the son of notary Jaume who worked as a physician. Jaume's family had originally been Jewish, but his father, Cresquas, a grain and money dealer based a few miles north in Avignon, had converted to Catholicism around 1460, taking the Christian name 'Pierre' and the surname 'Nostredame' the saint on whose day his conversion was solemnized.*"

Holmes repeated it slowly, "'Nostredame,' the saint on whose day his conversion was solemnized.'"

"Yes I got that."

"Which Notre Dame would inspire a Jew to convert in this area of France?"

"Which, you mean there are two?"

"No…yes, but originally there was only one."

"Mary Magdalene?" I queried. "Are you saying Mary Magdalene is Notre Dame?"

"Was Notre Dame. The day he converted must have been 22nd July, which is Mary Magdalene's feast day. And there are no specific days for the Virgin mother. Or I should say there are several but none as specific as that of the Magdalene."

"So Mary Magdalene is the Notre Dame he called himself after."

"Yes, they stole the title off her and invented the cult of the Mother Mary who is a minor character in the Gospels but a major character for the Church. That is why they removed the name Notre Dame-de-la-Mar and replaced it with the awkward, Saints Maries-de-la-Mer. She landed here and it was named Notre Dame-de-la-Mer, for no other reason than that is her title."

"Wait a minute does that mean the Church of Notre Dame de Paris is actually dedicated to Mary Magdalene?"

"That's a good point, Watson. Certainly it is said the Architects were Knights Templar who venerated the Magdalene."

"And Notre Dame de Chartes?"

"Probably, since they were both built in the twelfth century, when the Templars were at their height."

Holmes closed his book and rose from his chair. "We will leave later this afternoon. Now, I am going round to the telegraph office, I have a few questions for 'mon bon frère', and then to la librairie de Perrine to investigate further."

And with that he left me at the table. So I ordered a coffee and bread with their delicious Bayonne ham.

After packing I went round to the bookshop and found Holmes sitting on the floor reading and Perrine at her counter also reading surrounded by open books.

"Well my friends, have you any confirmation of your theory."

Holmes looked up, "Yes, a whole number of things and Perrine has some interesting findings."

She looked up. "Yes, the man responsible for the building of Notre Dame de Paris in 1163 was the Bishop of Paris, Maurice de Sully. His history shows links to the beliefs of the Templars who were just rising to their peak. For instance he converted a synagogue that was seized from the Jews of Paris, and duly consecrated it as a church dedicated to Mary Magdalene! So the Magdalene was foremost in his mind."

Holmes cut in, "But what do you think his attitude to the Virgin Mother was?" He answered his own question. "Sully forbade the celebration of her feast of the Immaculate Conception in his diocese."

"The immaculate conception?" I remembered. "Isn't that the subject of Leonardo's 'Virgin on the Rocks' that you found so funny?"

"Yes, like Leonardo, Sully did not think much of this weird idea that the Virgin was also born of a virgin. And Leonardo never described the lady in his painting as the Madonna; he called her La Nostra Signora, Italian for, Notre Dame."

"Are you suggesting the lady in that painting is the Magdalene?" I asked.

"You may be surprised," said Holmes. "But Perrine found another version of the Virgin of the Rocks. Show him."

"It is in the Musée des Beaux-arts in Caen," said Perrine.

"The main differences are the hair and the clothes," said Holmes. "The hair is now red like the Magdalene and beneath the blue cloak of the Madonna is the red dress of the Magdalene

And strangely the angel, whose wings are now very defined has red hair and the green and red clothes of the Magdalene."

""Does that suggest the setting in the painting is here in the Grotto where the Magdalene spent her last years?" I asked

"It seems so, it certainly is not Israel or Egypt, although what the babies and the angel are doing there, only Leonardo knows."

"What about Notre Dame de Chartes?" I asked.

"Here," said Perrine pushing one of the open books on her counter towards me. This is a plan of the famous Magdalene window in the Cathedral of Notre Dame de Chartes."

"You see," said Holmes, "it ignores all the huffing and puffing by officialdom and makes the Magdalene the sister of Lazarus, windows 8 to 10, and the person who perfumes

Jesus' feet, window 4. It also tells of a journey to Gaul, window 15 and her death in the arms of Maximin. I think it confirms that the Masons who built Notre Dame de Chartes were dedicating the building to Mary Magdalene, not the Virgin mother."

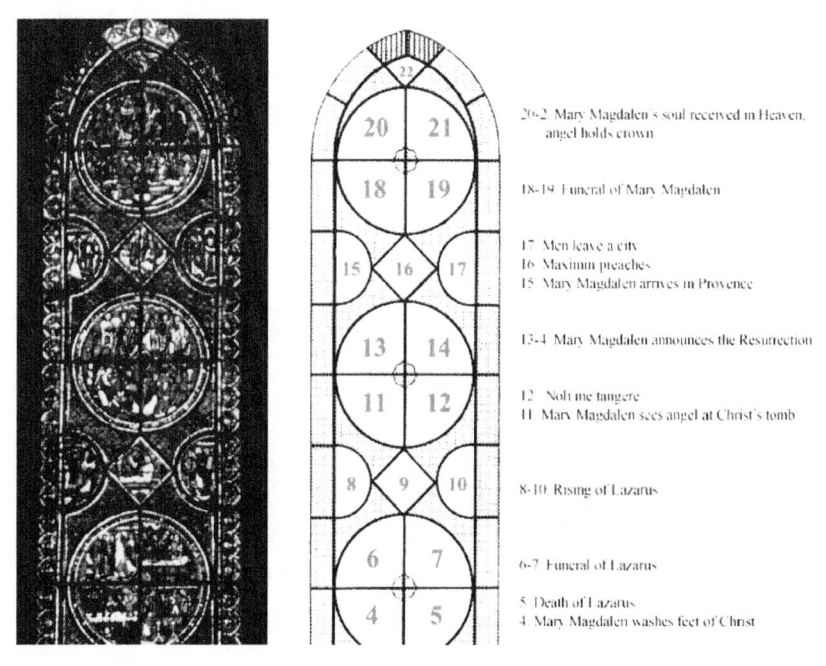

20-2 Mary Magdalen's soul received in Heaven, angel holds crown

18-19 Funeral of Mary Magdalen

17 Men leave a city
16 Maximin preaches
15 Mary Magdalen arrives in Provence

13-4 Mary Magdalen announces the Resurrection

12 Noli me tangere
11 Mary Magdalen sees angel at Christ's tomb

8-10 Rising of Lazarus

6-7 Funeral of Lazarus

5 Death of Lazarus
4 Mary Magdalen washes feet of Christ

"I think it is clear who the masons thought was Notre Dame when they built the two Cathedrals."

"I think it might also be true of Victor Hugo," added Perrine, "when he wrote the 'Hunchback of Notre Dame'. He was steeped in the French esoteric world. Remember Quasimodo is elected 'Pope of Fools. And who is the bad man in the story, the Catholic, Archdeacon Frollo."

"The clue to the Templars real allegiance lies with Templar Grand Master Jacques de Molay when he was burnt at the stake. The event occurred on a small Island in the Seine and he asked to be tied in such a way that as he was burning, he could face and pray to the Cathedral of Notre Dame as to him Notre Dame was not Jesus' virgin mother but the Magdalene."

"I must show you the postcard being sold here," said Holmes as he went to the counter where Perrine passed him one of the postcards from the rack behind her.

"Remember the statue in the church there. It did not mean much to us at the time but now after Perrine explained the story of the town, it becomes outrageous."

"Why?" I asked.

""See it says, Mary Jacob and Mary Salome and even the servant Sara, but no Mary Magdalene! All the stories about this place state that there were three Maries who landed here. But what used to be three is now two, Mary Jacobe and Mary Salome. Have they no shame, changing the name of the town, then removing the Magdalene from the boat?"

"That is strange."

"I tell you what is really strange," said Holmes. "One of the remaining images in the boat is clearly Mary Magdalene with her red hair and her jar at her feet. I wonder if the locals, when they were told to remove Mary Magdalene,

160

removed one of the others in defiance. If they did, well done chaps, for that you deserve a Navette. They keep the real story alive any way they can."

CHAPTER 26

Avignon

We said our goodbyes to Perrine and settled back in the small carriage we had hired to take us to Avignon where we were going to stay the night before travelling back to Narbonne.

We moved out of the flat grassland to more hilly terrain. The Rhone ran back to the sea on our left.

"Nostradamus' father worked in Avignon," Holmes remarked out of the blue. "I wonder how Debussy knows so much about the subject. Besides being a fabulous composer has he been secretly researching the subject?"

"Or one of his group has," I suggested

"Maybe the Church of St. Sulpice, which was a hotbed of Modernism, has information. Information that was in the Jericho Manuscript."

"It is interesting," I considered, "how your improvisations on the violin have such a similar feel to Debussy's music."

"It is probably just that he is a favourite of mine and so my subconscious copies it."

Nearing Avignon we passed over a small bridge and Holmes began to hum a tune. He certainly was a more mellow character since our journey began. I think Perrine might have been responsible for some of that as his humming turned into song.

"Sur le Pont d'Avignon, L'on y danse, l'on y danse,
Sur le Pont d'Avignon, L'on y danse tous en rond."

"Is there a bridge in Avignon?" I asked.

"There are quite a few but I think Pont d'Avignon is officially Pont Saint-Bénézet, that dates back to the 15th century. I was told the dance actually took place under the bridge and not on the bridge, sous, not sur."

"Have you been here before?" I asked.

"Yes, remember, some two or three years ago I was employed by the Comte de Rochefort, to investigate the disappearance of his wife."

"No, I don't remember. How did it turn out?"

"I am afraid I can't tell you because he swore me to secrecy to protect the family name."

The great walls of Avignon appeared and the coach turned in through the gateway and along the narrow streets to the Hôtel Mirande where we, and the suitcase disembarked. We checked in and Holmes took me straight out to see the Pope's Palace, a formidable structure that seemed to be built to withstand attack as much as to perform religious duties.

"In the fourteenth century," said Holmes, "seven French Popes resided here. Pope Clement bought the town from Joanna of Naples. It stayed in the control of the Popes, like the Vatican, until the French Revolution when it became part of France."

To our left was a bell tower with a massive gold statue of the Virgin Mother sitting on top. We asked about it in the tourist shop. We were told the Romanesque church of Notre Dame des Doms was built way back in 1150. This was abandoned and allowed to deteriorate. And then suddenly it was renovated in 1840. The new bell tower was erected and placed on top was the massive gilded statue of the Virgin Mary. We left the shop and looked back at that enormous gilded statue.

"Is this a case of a Notre Dame Church being allowed to deteriorate," said Holmes, "and then later renovated and a new massive Notre Dame placed on top to squash the old Notre Dame out of existence?"

It left us with a hollow feeling in our stomachs just considering the possibility. The Magdalene must have been an extraordinary woman, but her legacy has been wiped out and no end of slanders and insults aimed at her.

The mood had been dampened at dinner in the Hotel.

"If we think the Magdalene was hard done by," I considered. "At least she is in the Gospels. Her brother Lazarus was nearly wiped out completely if it was not for the addition of John's Gospel."

"Too true, John's Gospel, literally raised him from the dead,' smiled Holmes.

"Tell me what do you make of the story of his resurrection?"

Holmes thought for a while, "What did I tell you when we confronted the legendry beast of the Baskervilles?"

I remembered what Holmes had said, "If we are dealing with forces outside the ordinary laws of nature, there is an end to our investigation."

"Lazarus' resurrection certainly appears to be outside the laws of nature," said Holmes.

"But you were the only one who refused to accept the spectral hound being unearthly and outside the laws of nature, because it left footprints," I said. "So is there any explanation that brings the Lazarus event down to earth?"

"Yes there is."

Holmes took me by surprise with such a definite response.

"What is it?"

"Wait a moment," Holmes got up. "Order me a cognac."

He went up and came back with the tatters, which was once his Bible. He took a sip of his cognac and opened a tab and read.

"So when he heard that Lazarus was sick, he stayed where he was two more days, and then he said to his disciples, "Let us go back to Judea. Then Thomas (also known as Didymus) said to the rest of the disciples, "Let us also go, that we may die with him."

"What can Thomas possibly mean by that? Do they all want to go and catch his disease and die too? Or are they thinking to go there and commit suicide and die with their comrade?"

"Surely not! That makes no sense."

"I can give you one possible answer, said Holmes. Do you remember the Isle of Wight tallow chandler murder?"

"Yes the skull and crossbones and all the candles around the body." I remembered. "Of course it was my friend the very same Reverend Adams who helped you solve it."

"Yes and you remember he swore us to secrecy when he told us how and where the skull and crossed bones came from."

"The Masonic Hall in Ryde."

"It was used in third degree initiation," said Holmes, "where the novitiate is laid down dead in a shroud and a skull and cross bones above his head. Then while one Master offers the secret grip, the novitiate is hinged up from the grave by the Masters, whispering the magic words, as they resurrect him back to life as a Master Mason."

"A death and rebirth ritual?" I gasped.

"That would certainly make sense as to why the others would want to die to be born again to the next stage of initiation."

"And remember when Jesus is told Lazarus is dead," continued Holmes, "he waits another two days. Why? Because in the ancient Orphic mysteries the initiate is in Hades for three days. So it looks like the initiate has to remain in the grave for three days."

I sat there for a moment, then picked up my cognac and gulped it down and waved to the waiter.

"Garçon. Un autre de ceux-ci s'il vous plaît, et faites-en un double."

CHAPTER 27

The Crucifixion

The luxurious silk sheets of the Hôtel Mirande made sleep such a pleasure that we woke late. We had just a few moments to pack and head for the Diligence to Narbonne. Holmes left his case with me and made a divergence to the telegraph office. He returned with the yellow paper in hand.

The coach arrived and we boarded. The driver and helper loaded Holmes' suitcase and I am sure the springs sunk down a further six inches with the weight.

We juddered down to Narbonne without much talking. We were excited with the thought of coming face to face with the Dominicans and seeing the missing Jericho manuscript. Holmes just glanced at his telegram but did not discuss it with me.

We checked back into our old hotel and made for the Abbey. Holmes knocked on the door and we were again received by the same novice and again shown into the waiting room. After half an hour the Novice returned.

"Il ne peut pas vous voir ce soir il dirige les vêpres. Il faudra que ce soit après le tiers."

"He will see us tomorrow after terce? Quelle heure est-il?" asked Holmes.

"Neuf heures et demi," said the novice.
And two very disappointed Englishmen left the Abbey.

We dressed for dinner and just a few steps into the old city, we found an interesting restaurant with outside tables, au Coq Hardi. I obviously ordered the coq au vin, which was absolutely delicious with the local sausage in addition to the traditional lardoons. To be different, Holmes had the côté d'agneau, which he said was equally delicious. Along with a demi of local wine, it was a fine meal that rekindled our spirits.

"You haven't told me of your telegram," said I. "Was it Mycroft?"

"It was." He pulled it out of his pocket.

"Did you set him the conundrum about crucifixion?"

"I did," said Holmes smiling.

"Did it cost a fortune?"

"Not at all. See, eight words did it." He passed over the receipt with his question.

'THOUGHT EXPERIMENT STOP BUILD A CRUCIFIX STOP EXPLAIN SPARTACUS 6000'

"And did he explain the six thousand?"

"That he did."

"Well?"

"It is all a matter of translation. The word being translated as Crucifix is Stauros. The word stauros comes from the same root as the English 'stand'. In classical Greek, stauros meant an upright stake, on which anything might be hung. In the literature of that time it never meant two pieces of timber placed across one another at any angle, but always one piece alone."

"My Goodness. That means…"

"That there is no reason to believe Jesus was on a cross at all; nor that the six thousand Spartacus slaves crucified on the Appian Way, were on crosses. In fact, it would almost be impossible. Impaling would be on nothing more than a spear or javelin, like a hog roast. The feet could be on the ground. Nobody was going to rescue these people, and if the spear came out of the neck or the mouth it would be horrific even to a Roman. I suspect when the sentence was carried out at an official execution the feet would be tied or nailed each side of the stake so that the victim did not slide down killing him quickly when the stake pierced the diaphragm and destroyed the vital organs of the chest. He would suffer the agony for hours, so as a mercy killing the legs would be broken to finish off the victim. Just as it says in the Bible. Whereas breaking the legs of a person on the cross would have no effect whatsoever."

"I'm glad we finished dinner before we discussed this. I am even now feeling a little queasy."

Holmes called the waiter. "Garçon, un cognac pour mon ami."

The cognac certainly helped to settle my stomach enough for me to return to the subject.

"So you have come to the conclusion that Jesus was staked?"

"No, I think he was on a cross. And I think he was nailed through the hands. It is in too many images."

"But we proved nails in the hands would not hold the weight." I protested.

"Unless there was no weight on the hands because the footrest was a flat platform."

CHAPTER 28

Chrestos

We woke in the morning to be welcomed by a strange brooding yellow sky. The sun was red with no real power. It was like a bad omen for the coming day. At coffee they told us it was a sandstorm in the Sahara sending sand into the upper atmosphere, and the southerly wind had blown it across the Mediterranean.

When we came out of the hotel, there was a light dusting of sand on everything. We went back to the Abbey and knocked and we were again received by the same novice and again shown into the same waiting room. After three quarters of an hour a new man appeared.

"Monsieur l'Abbé?" asked Holmes.

"Oui Monsieur."

"Saviez-vous que nous avons appelé pour parler avec les deux frères qui avaient du boeuf à Paris," said Holmes.

"Oui monsieur voudriez-vous me raconter toute l'histoire."

Holmes did as the Abbot asked giving every detail of the story from the killing in Saint Saviour's to the death of Elmeny. When he finished the Abbot just sat there with his hands almost together as if in prayer.

Homes broke the silence. "Can we talk with Jaques and Nicolas to see if they can help our investigation?"

"No I don't think so," replied the Abbot.

"Why not?" asked Holmes.

"Because they are not here."

"Where are they?"

"They are at the Monastère de Prouilhe."

"The Monastère de Prouilhe? The one you have just come from on the other side of Carcassonne," Holmes said in disbelief.

"The same," said the Abbot. "In fact they travelled with me, but stayed when I left."

"Is the manuscript here? Can we at least see that?"

"I am afraid I know nothing about any manuscript," said the Abbot as he rose from the chair.

"Can we go to the Monastère de Prouilhe and see them?" Holmes asked.

"Of course," said the Abbot as he left the room and the novice waved his arm from us towards the front door.

Disappointed, but at least we had time to catch the diligence to Carcassonne. Again we told the Hotel we were leaving and not staying that night, which infuriated them, as it was the second time we had pulled the same trick. They insisted we pay fifty percent of the rooms for such a late cancellation.

The coach was not leaving till two so we sat next to the stop in an outdoor restaurant, the two of us and the suitcase.

"There was more in that telegram than just the crucifixion story," I noted.

"Yes I sent another after the information we discovered chez Perrine's."

"What was it about?" I asked.

"It is very long winded to explain."

"Well we have three hours to kill now and another four in the coach."

"Okay, but it will take all of those seven hours to explain."

"Don't tell me he wrote you a telegram that takes seven hours to read?" I teased.

"No, I just asked him to look up a name in the encyclopaedias," Holmes began. "A name that could be the missing Chrestos."

"Your profile has produced a potential individual for Suetonius's Chrestos?"

"The contradictions I pointed out in the Gospels have added up to suggesting a single person."

"Really?"

"Remember contradiction one has Jesus functioning in Galilee and collecting his disciples by the Sea of Galilee, who leave their employ on a whim. But this is flatly contradicted in another Gospel that has Jesus functioning in Judea where he collects the same disciples who are followers of the Baptist, and take days to decide to join Jesus. Contradiction two has Jesus arrested by a few Temple guards, which is contradicted by an arrest by the full Roman Jerusalem garrison.

"Contradiction three has Jesus brought before High Priest Caiaphas where Peter denies Jesus in the courtyard; While another has him brought to High Priest Annas where Peter denies him in Annas' courtyard.

"Four has Jesus accused of blasphemy by the High Priest but when brought before Pilate he is accused of not paying taxes and claiming to be king of the Jews, which does not follow the text as Jesus says render unto Caesar that which is Caesars. While these are not the only contradiction that suggest two separate people being talked about, they are the most obvious."

"My Goodness you are not going to suggest there were two different people?"

"I'm not going to suggest it. It was you. You suggested two people right at the beginning, don't you remember?"

"So now you are going to blame me so that I get burnt at the stake. Just like you used my name to get me nearly chopped by Madam guillotine."

"I can see why people read your books," said Holmes. "You can make high drama out of nothing."

"Nothing!" I gasped. "Nothing. I don't think you realize how explosive the information is you are unravelling. The population of Britain go to church every Sunday and you undermining the whole story."

"Why do we need to tell anyone? It appears many people, from the Templars to the Rosicrucians seem to know the monumental secret. So we will just join the ranks of the those in the know."

"Very well, it's a secret. You realise I have been looking forward to writing 'Holmes takes a Holiday' now my hands are tied."

"Not by me they aren't," said Holmes.

"Yes because you have put my name on the theory."

"Well I had a totally different theory, but the more I discovered the more I realised, you had the right answer."

"The one time I am right and you are wrong about anything, I can't tell people."

"Do you want me to go on, or not?" asked Holmes.

"Go on, go on; let me hear how right I was; I'll worry about my reputation once we get back to London."

"Right," said Holmes taking from his case Josephus one and a half. "So if the peace loving Christos is one of these people, is the militant Chrestos, the other? Was Jesus the person functioning in Judea while Chrestos was functioning in Galilee? Was the mystic Jesus arrested by Temple guards on a charge of blasphemy, while, the militant Chrestos was arrested by the full garrison of Roman soldiers and taken to Pilate on a charge of rebellion and refusing to pay taxes? Surely Chrestos must have been a really famous Jewish militant, somehow associated with Galilee. He must have had a massive following, as his ideas and fame spread all the way to Rome, where his militant followers caused enough trouble in AD 49 for all Jews to be banished by Claudius. He also needs to start functioning at least twenty years before Claudius to have time to spread his ideas throughout Israel and then on to the Jews of Rome. And he must have refused to pay Roman tax and claim to be King of the Jews?"

"That's quite a full profile. Is there such a person, perhaps one of the rebels you listed before who wore diadems?"

"None of them but there is a different person who fits this profile perfectly. A man Josephus tells us was a claimant to the throne, who started spreading his message thirty years before Claudius in 6 AD. Here in my notes is Josephus very words which confirm my profile."

Holmes read from his notebook the list.
"The nation was infected with his doctrine'
'He was a clever Rabbi'
"He stated they were cowards if they would endure to pay a tax to the Romans."
'He was author of the fourth branch of Jewish philosophy.'
'He stirred his followers to rebellion.
'and Josephus claims he was responsible for the war.
'They, 'his followers' have an inviolable attachment to liberty, and say that God is to be their only Ruler and Lord.'

'They do not value dying any kinds of death, nor indeed do they heed the deaths of their relations and friends, nor can any such fear make them call any man lord.'

"A clever rabbi who begins functioning in 6 AD; who was against paying taxes to the Romans, who created a whole new branch of Jewish Philosophy, which spread like wild fire; whose followers believe in an afterlife, which means they face death as martyrs and do not call any ruler Lord. On top of all this our man is often referred to simply as, the Galilean! This has to be Judas the Galilean."

"I don't know that I have even heard of him, although the name does ring a bell."

"Because he is mentioned in the Bible," said Holmes. "So when I realised this was possibly our man I looked him up in Perrine's French encyclopaedia but the text was nonsense. So I wrote to Mycroft to look him up in British encyclopaedias."

"Did they mention him? What did Mycroft send you?"

Holmes opened the telegram. "They do, here are two extraordinary statements from British encyclopaedias that Mycroft found about him." Holmes read: *"Judas was a Jewish leader who led an armed resistance to the census imposed for Roman tax purposes by Quirinius in Judaea Province around 6 AD. The revolt was crushed brutally by the Romans. These events are discussed by Josephus in his book 'Jewish Wars.'*

"And this one Mycroft found in the Jewish Encyclopaedia.

'Judas was leader of a popular revolt against the Romans at the time when the first census was taken in Judea, in which revolt he perished and his followers were dispersed.'

"This is the same extraordinary nonsense that was in the French encyclopaedias!" said Holmes.

"What is so extraordinary, they seem pretty straight forward to me?"

"You think so? Well let me tell you, there is hardly a word of these supposed expert opinions that is true, except perhaps: *'These events are discussed by Josephus in his book, 'The Jewish War.'* Yes, they are discussed by Josephus but not in the *'Jewish War'* book, but more so in his book *'Antiquities'* and anyway in no book by Josephus can one find that he: *'led an armed resistance to the census'*. Or *'The revolt was crushed brutally by the Romans.'* Or *'In which revolt he perished and his followers were dispersed.'"*

"It could just be bad or sloppy research?"

"If it is sloppy research it has to be very sloppy because there are only some ten pages in all of Josephus that mentions the Galilean, so if you cannot read ten pages and transcribe them correctly you have to be either pretty dumb, or blind, or very deceitful."

"So what are you saying is the truth."

"For a start there is no mention of Judas dying anywhere in Josephus. For all we know he could have died in his bed of old age. And secondly let me read you from the end of the 'War' book, the actual nature of the revolt. *'At that time the Sicarii combined against those prepared to submit to Rome, and in every way treated them as enemies, looting their property, rounding up their cattle, and setting their dwellings on fire: because they declared they were no better than foreigners, throwing away in this cowardly fashion the freedom won by the Jews at such cost, and avowedly choosing slavery under the Romans.'* So the revolt against Roman tax was not an armed uprising against the Romans but instead he persuaded *many* of the people of Judea not to register. And those that did were visited by the Sicarii attacking any major person who collaborated with the Romans, *'Looting their property, rounding up their cattle, and setting their dwellings on fire.'* So the violence was not aimed at the Romans but at wealthy Jewish collaborators."

"And that is why you suggest the rich fled Israel and came here to Narbonne," I added.

"Also this is not the section about the Galilean it is fifty years on, but Josephus wrote that this was all *recorded earlier* in the book, but it is not. So I think we can safely say that there was a cut in the earlier section on Judas the Galilean. This is also confirmed when one looks at his 'Antiquities' book where you get this: *'The sons of Judas of Galilee were now slain: I mean of that Judas who caused the people to revolt, when Quirinius came to take an account of the estates of the Jews, as we have shown in a foregoing book.'*

"The foregoing book was the 'War' book?"

"Yes this book about this actual period," said Holmes holding up the full book. "But we have no mention of these sons in the War book, or what they did to get themselves slain. But clearly it was once in here, but is no longer."

Holmes held up his torn piece of Antiquities. "There are whole numbers of key events in this little scrap of 'Antiquities', about the war that are not in the 'War' book, which is supposed to be just about the War."

"For example," I asked.

"The destruction of Herod's army, the marriage of Herodius and the beheading of John the Baptist. There are things that are open to dispute but what cannot be disputed," said Holmes seriously, "is that the 'War' book has been edited to remove information about the Galilean. The question is why?"

"Why?"

"Yes; why would anyone tamper with Josephus and edit out information about Judas the Galilean? It is quite obvious why the Baptist would be cut out of the book, if Josephus had written things that disagreed with the biblical story. And it is equally obvious why Jesus brother James would be cut if again it disagreed with the Bible text. But, why cut out the activities of Judas the Galilean, who superficially has absolutely nothing at all to do with the Jesus story? It can only be that Judas the Galilean's story does have something that clashes dramatically with the Gospel story! And it is clearly something of very great magnitude."

"Yes, but here is our coach," I said, "and I think your object of great magnitude needs to be hoisted aboard."

Together we lifted Holmes suitcase onto the luggage shelf and got into the coach breathless.

CHAPTER 29

Who Killed Chrestos?

As we left Narbonne and headed inland I found myself trying to comprehend what was going on.

"What are you doing?" asked Holmes.

"What am I doing?"

"You're shaking your head."

"Am I? I didn't realise I was doing it. I think it was Freud's subconscious doing it."

"You will be talking to yourself soon," said Holmes.

"Soon! I'm doing it now. I mean, with all the Biblical Scholars in the world, from Australia to America, you in ten days unravel the whole blessed thing. And what have you got, six books."

"And two expensive telegrams."

"Okay your books are a damn nuisance but these others have whole libraries of information."

"I can only assume that they look at documents for what is written in them," said Holmes, "whereas I have been looking at documents for what is not written in them, what must have been there but is now missing. It is a method I have used often. Remember the Tufnell Park Christmas affair?

"Yes, I do."

"The table was laid for dinner and Inspector Lestrade counted all the plates for the numbers who had sat down."

"And, if I remember rightly, Holmes, he even made a good guess as to who was sitting where by the portions on the plates."

"That's right Watson, everything was laid out, spoons had served potatoes and another had served the brussel sprouts."

"And Lastrade counted the turkey slices on the plate to decide who were the big meat eaters, which is usually the males."

"Yes," said Holmes. "All very good. But the one thing he missed, was…"

"The missing item from the table," I added.

"Which," said Holmes, "turned out to be the most important bit of information."

"That's right, the carving knife. The murder weapon."

"So what is missing is as important as what is there. And the list of what is missing from Josephus grows by the day. From Josephus alone we have missing the death of the Galilean. We have missing when and why two of his sons were caught and killed. Also missing unbelievably is the expulsion of the Jews from Rome, which in fact dates from the same time as the sons of the Galilean were killed. Were they captured in Rome, or Israel, and were they in anyway involved in the atrocity that caused the Jews to be expelled. And even worse, missing is one of the most disastrous events, that occurred in Rome and blamed by Nero on a Jew."

"What's that?"

"The Great Fire of 64 AD just two years before the first events of the Jewish war and blamed on either Christos or Chrestos."

"Tacitus writes, that of Rome's fourteen districts, ten were left in scorched ruin, only four escaped damage." I remembered.

"After the war," added Holmes," "when Josephus arrived in Rome and sat down to write, they must have still been rebuilding parts of the city all around him, so it is hard to imagine the event slipped his mind. And it is not that he does not mention Nero, he writes quite a bit about him. But the Great Fire; nothing. Surely all logic tells us it was there but has been spirited away."

"Interesting," I observed, "that what is missing is as important as what is there."

"Of course there is one other method I have used which is standard practise."

"Which is?"

"I have kept the four witness statements separate, as even the most dim-witted detective would do; and have compared them to see if there are contradictions and if so are they by fault or design."

"Damn me Holmes, I'm surprised they have not burnt you as a witch already."

"I, the witch? All I am doing is observing, but who but a witch could cast a spell that makes all the encyclopaedias in the world write that 'the Galilean died in 6 AD as reported by Josephus,' when it is not. And who but a witch could make academics not ask 'who is Chrestos?' when they are confronted by him in Suetonius. I tell you the witches have burnt, cut and edited books to protect their bizarre rituals that end in the chant of Amen."

I looked around at the other four passengers and hoped they could not speak English.

"Do be careful who you are calling a Witch."

"Why, you had no problem in calling me one."

I raised my hands apologetically. "I withdraw my assertion, you are not a Witch, you are simply a seeker after truth."

"I forgive you, my son," said Holmes absolving me. "And for your information I would not be a witch I would be a Warlock."

"I stand corrected on every count." Then a thought struck me and I saw a stumbling block in Holmes theory.

"If I may be allowed to raise a small point from my humble position?"

"Feel free," smiled Holmes.

"Now you say there is nowhere in Josephus that says when the Galilean was killed?"

"Correct."

"So the encyclopaedias could be right and he died in 6 AD. There is nothing that says the contrary"

"No, the Galilean never died in 6 AD."

"How do you know, if it is not reported, it could be anytime."

"This is a passage from the start of the War about his son. *One Menachem, the son of that Judas, who was called the Galilean, took some of the men of note with him, and retired to Masada, where he broke open King Herod's armory, and gave arms not only to his own people, but to other robbers also.*'

"So Menachem leads a team to climb the mountaintop of Masada around 67 AD and destroys the Roman garrison there."

"So how does that tell you how the Galilean died?"

"Not how, but when," said Holmes. "Do you think a seventy year old could climb up that mountain and still have enough energy to raise his sword against the Romans?"

"Ah, I see what you mean."

"Have a guess at Menachem's age," asked Holmes.

"Well, mid thirties sounds probable, say 36."

"Okay take 36 away from 67 the date of the attack."

"36 from 67 leaves 31," I reckoned.

"So by your calculation, Menachem was born around 31 AD. Therefore the Galilean could not have died in 6 AD otherwise it would have been his ghost who impregnated his wife twenty-five years later. And as I do not believe in ghosts I suggest he was alive when he performed this act of impregnation around 30 to 31 AD, and therefore probably died in 32 AD. How odd is this, that Jesus is claimed to have been crucified by Pontius Pilate in 32 AD."

"Slow down, Holmes. So you are suggesting again that Pilate killed Chrestos, the Galilean, not Jesus."

"Yes because in 32 AD, John the Baptist was still alive, so Jesus had not even started his ministry."

"So the Galilean is dead and Jesus is alive in 33 AD?" I considered.

"Is that still a bit too big a jump of logic for you? Well just remember, when Josephus mentioned the appointment of Caiaphas as High Priest, he added: *'Caiaphas became a high priest during a turbulent period.'* So this *'turbulent period'*, seems to have been brought to an end by bringing in a different type of Governor to the province of Judea. Pontius Pilate's title, is not governor but *Praefectus*, or Prefect, a military term reflecting the fact that the province was turbulent and Pilate's chief task was to bring law and order to the land."

"Enter Pontius Pilate."

"And how did Pilate bring this turbulent period to an end? By crucifying the peace-loving Jesus? Obviously not! It had to be the destruction of the rebel army and the capture and killing of their leader, Judas the Galilean. And then their follows a period of peace for Jesus to function in, till the sons of Judas become of age to continue the battle."

Holmes sat back in his seat with a satisfied grin as we sighted the turrets of Carcassonne.

"Maybe I should have slept through the journey," I said, "because after that lot I don't think I'm going to sleep tonight."

CHAPTER 30

Champagne

We checked into the Hôtel de la Cité, which was once a medieval church that local stonemasons had built into the South-western wall that surrounds Carcassonne. I changed for dinner and lumbered down to the restaurant. I was worn out by the journey and the body of information my brain had tried to digest, but there was Holmes in the hotel bar as sprightly as a spring chicken with his glass of Pastis comparing his Eusebius with the Bible and taking down notes. He looked up as he saw me coming.

"What will you have?" he asked.

"A new brain if they have one."

"Where's your 'jour de vie' Watson. Garçon, un champagne pour mon ami."

"You may have just been doing your crossword but my brain has been at the end of a battering ram."

Holmes laughed, and a few sips of champagne did raise my spirits.

"Your champagne has a history you know Watson."

"Really what is it?" And that was my big mistake because I opened the door for Holmes to dive in. He took out his notebook and immediately embarked on a full frontal assault.

"The Count of Champagne, was a founding father of the Templars. Listen to this: *'Troyes was the seat of the court of the Count of Champagne and it was Chrétian of Troyes who wrote one of the earliest Grail romances, which figured the Templars as the guardians of the Grail.'* That is just like

Wagner's story of Parsifal. But even more interesting is that the Count made Troyes, a centre of Cabalistic and esoteric studies as early as eleventh century. Behind it was a Rabbi probably known even today by Orthodox Jews as Solomon of Troyes, or Rabbi Rashid. Rashid was author of a comprehensive commentary on the Talmud, which has been included in every edition of the Talmud since its first printing. Now we know very well what is in the Talmud don't we?"

"Do we?" I pleaded but Homes was at his notebook and was going to tell me.

"'*The Sages of the Synagogue, succeeding in capturing Jeschu, who was then led before the Great and Little Sanhedrin, by whom he was condemned to be stoned to death and his dead body was hung on a tree.*'"

And this is the ritual of stoning I found in Deuteronomy.

'*If a man guilty of a capital offense is put to death and his body hung on a tree, you must not leave his body on the tree overnight. Be sure to bury him that same day, because anyone who is hung on a tree is under God's curse. You must not desecrate the land the Lord your God is giving you as an inheritance.*'"

"So after stoning the body is hung on a tree?"

"Yes, and what is interesting is that there appears to be a residual of the event in Acts because it says: '*Whom they slew and hung on a tree.*' So he is slain before he is hung on a tree as with stoning. Has this slipped through the editing process to reveal a truth? And it is not alone; Peter actually accuses the Sanhedrin of Jesus' death in Acts 5. '*The God of our ancestors raised Jesus from the dead – whom you killed by hanging him on a tree.*' What do you make of that Watson?"

"I order a champagne and you give me a lecture on Champagne. If I order the lamb for dinner will you give me a never ending lecture on the symbol of the Lamb of God and how carrots represent the donkeys in the stable?"

"So endeth the third lesson," said Holmes, calming me with his hands. He stood up for an attack on the restaurant.

"Camarades, avançons pour manger."

I must have been hungry because after finishing my duck a l'orange I felt a lot cheerier. Holmes was still tackling his oeufs farcis au crabe, a much simpler way of eating crab.

"I am going to order a tarte tropézienne with my cognac," I said, "which I think will give me the energy to ask you a question, which I know the answer will have us here till midnight."

"Midnight, then I will order a Tarte Tatin with my Courvoisier to get me through."

Once we had devoured our desserts we retired into the bar to sit on the armchairs and Holmes placed his Eusebius on the table. Luckily for the other clients Holmes asked for a cigarette instead of going up for his pipe. The waiter lit his cigarette and Holmes took a puff, blew the smoke up into the air and looked at the cigarette.

"A Gauloises," he remarked. "Do you remember it was the very first clue that began this long journey of discovery?"

"That's right, you found the tip by the tree outside Canon Lilly's rectory."

"My, what a time we have had," mused Holmes.

"A holiday to remember, aye Holmes."

"Yes indeed. So fire away Watson or we will be here all night."

"Right," I gathered my thoughts. "Now you have virtually proven that Pilate killed the Galilean and that Jesus was alive after Pilate left Judea."

"Yes, that is true."

"And I see you are leaning towards the Jewish idea that Jesus was stoned to death by the Jewish council, the Sanhedrin."

Holmes nodded. "Who else would know the truth of what happened but the Israelites themselves."

"But you have several times mentioned that you do believe he was crucified with nails in the hands. Does that mean you believe in the resurrection?"

"You see this book on Ecclesiastic history." Holmes picked up Eusebius from the table. "Bishop Eusebius attacks several heretical groups and the most common are Christians who believe Jesus was a great man but not a God. This goes right back to an Ebionite community who we know of as existing in Israel before the Roman War."

Homes opened Eusebius at a tab and read:

"The ancients called them Ebionites because they held a poor opinion concerning Christ. For they considered him a plain and common man, who was justified only because of his superior virtue and was the fruit of the intercourse of a man with Mary.' So the earliest followers did not believe Jesus was a God but just a good man and they did not believe he was born of a virgin but by normal intercourse with a man."

"Much like the Moslem belief," I added.

"Indeed," said Holmes.

"So, like the Ebionites you believe Jesus was not a supernatural being and was subject to the laws of nature."

"Yes."

"I think I would probably believe the same. So what is the crucifixion you say Jesus underwent?"

"You know my dictum about the impossible," said Holmes.

"Oh yes," I remembered his saying, "Once you eliminate the impossible, whatever remains, no matter how improbable, must be the truth."

Holmes pulled his notebook out from his jacket pocket.

"And I think the improbable truth is revealed in John's Gospel 19:38. *At the place where Jesus was crucified, there was a garden, and in the garden a new tomb.'*

"And they place the body in this garden tomb,' I added.

"Describe the tomb to me," asked Holmes.

"Me? Well it is in the garden, a sort of cave with a door which is stone and rolls into place."

"That is exactly how it is described in Matthew 27. *'Joseph took the body, wrapped it in a clean linen cloth, and placed it in his own new tomb that he had cut out of the rock. He rolled a big stone in front of the entrance to the tomb and went away."*

"So my description is correct," I said.

"Yes. But how many homes in Jerusalem have gardens? This is not Maida Vale where every house has a little garden. Gardens in the Middle East are generally in Palaces. Agreed?"

"Yes."

"And how many of these houses in Jerusalem with gardens have tombs in them?"

"I've no idea." I replied.

"And how many of these tombs have rolling stone doors?"

"Not many, I would imagine."

"Can you think of one other?"

"No." Then a thought struck me. "Wait yes. I see where you are going with this. The garden in Bethany."

"Yes!" said Holmes. "That garden has a tomb where Lazarus lived out his death and resurrection ritual and it had a rolling stone door."

"Are you suggesting the crucifixion took place in the garden of Bethany and the body placed in the same tomb used by Lazarus?"

"After three days in the tomb Mary finds the tomb empty and runs to tell the other, who run back. So the tomb has to be close enough to their home for people to run backwards and forwards to. And then later Mary meets Jesus in the garden and mistakes him for….?

"A gardener!" I exclaimed.

"What would a gardener be doing around the site of execution? Arranging the flowers?"

"So you think the crucifixion took place in Bethany. Why?"

"I can only think that it is part of a death and resurrection ritual that involves being nailed to a cross that possibly represents the four elements of air, earth, fire and water."

"Would people do that to themselves?"

"There are far worse initiation ceremonies in the world. And remember he is again three days in Hades like the Orphic mysteries."

I shook my head. "I'm not sure I can accept this theory it seems too drastic."

Holmes smiled. "Once you eliminate the impossible, whatever remains, no matter how improbable, must be the truth."

"Yes, but have yourself nailed to a cross?"

Look," said Holmes, "Presumably there are funeral directors in ancient Israel, as the body is ritually unclean, so requires washing and having the hair and nails cut. But who carries out this process for Jesus?

"If I remember rightly it is Arimathea and Nicodemus, right?"

"Right. Why would a couple of rich, bigwigs like Joseph of Arimathea and Nicodemus, suddenly turn up with all the trappings of funeral directors to perform this unclean process?"

"I know how complex the Jewish laws are about what is clean and what is unclean as I have several Jewish patients."

"So I was asking myself," said Holmes. "What were they actually doing in the tomb? The answer lies in the moment shown in hundreds of paintings called *Noli me tangere*.

"It is the moment when Mary Magdalene finds the tomb empty and turns and sees someone."

"Who she mistakes for the gardener," I added.

"But what exactly is happening in these *Noli me tangere*, paintings? Perhaps I can explain with a quote about the initiation of the Essenes into higher degrees." Holmes read from Josephus.

"'They are divided into four classes, according to their duration in the training, and the later-joiners are so inferior to the earlier-joiners that if they should touch them, the latter wash themselves off as if they have mingled with a foreigner.' What does *Noli me tangere* mean?"

"Do not touch me!" I exclaimed.

"Why? Because he has been initiated to a higher level. 'Noli me tangere' has no other logical explanation and the church even suggest Jesus says this because he has moved to a higher level. What higher level can it be other than a higher level of initiation."

"Goodness me. That does sound feasible, it's just the crucifixion bit that I find hard to accept. That he used the same tomb Lazarus had used certainly seems likely."

"Not 'had used', was going to use," said Holmes.

"What does that mean?" I asked.

"Jesus could not initiate Lazarus if he had not already been initiated himself."

"So you are suggesting he went through this process before Lazarus."

"And before he had any disciples, which explains why they are not at the crucifixion only the Bethany family as is recorded in John. *'Near the cross of Jesus stood his mother, his mother's sister, Mary the wife of Clopas, and Mary Magdalene.'*"

'Wait a minute, are you suggesting the crucifixion happened at the beginning of his ministry?"

"Let me show you a report by Eusebius in chapter seven where, in attacking a heretical group he makes the most massive error."

Holmes turned to his Eusebius and read:

"For the things that they have dared to say concerning the passion of the Saviour are put into the fourth consulship of Tiberius, which occurred in the seventh year of his reign; at which time it is plain that Pilate was not yet ruling in Judea, if the testimony of Josephus is to be believed, who clearly shows in the above mentioned work that Pilate was made Procurator of Judea by Tiberius in the twelfth year of his reign.'"

"So what has he said that is so damning?" I asked.

"He is saying these critics are stating the crucifixion happened at a date that must be wrong because Pilate had not yet arrived in Israel."

"The seventh year of Tiberius reign makes it 21 AD."

"And that is the date Jesus was crucified according to these critics. And you realize why this statement would be passed over by Biblical Scholars."

I thought about it for a moment. "Because if they believe Jesus existed then they think Pilate was involved with his death, so they think Eusebius' criticism is correct."

"But of course it is not," said Holmes. "The truth is that the ritual crucifixion occurred at the beginning of Jesus ministry before Pilate arrived in Judea, not at the end and so these particular critics had it absolutely right."

"I wonder who they were who knew all this about the crucifixion."

"Probably the *blaspheming Jews* from this very area of the Languedoc?"

"And maybe those who put the stations of the cross round the wrong way to have the tomb at the beginning."

CHAPTER 31

The Dominicans

Next morning we ordered a four-wheeler to take us to the Monastère de Prouilhe, a one-hour drive from Carcassonne. The sun was shining and one could smell the flowers of the meadows. Luckily for the horses it was relatively flat so they managed us and the case reasonably well. As we approached Prouilhe it became a little more taxing and the fields turned to vineyards. Then left along a path, which opened the view to the impressive Monastère. A gilded sign announced 'Notre-Dame-de-Prouille' which made us think. We told the cab to wait. We knocked on the door and it was opened by a nun. We asked to see the Abbé and she showed us into a waiting room. Holmes picked up a leaflet from the table and read it to me:

"First foundation of Saint Dominic, the monastery of Prouilhe constitutes the cradle of the order of the Dominicans. It played a major role in the active defence of Catholic doctrine in the Middle Ages and, as such, is one of the most important royal monasteries of the Ancien Régime. It all started when Saint Dominic Guzman, originally from Spain, began his preaching in the Cathar country. He had in 1208 an apparition of the Virgin Mary who presents herself under the name of Notre Dame de la Rosary. Prouilhe became the symbol of the spiritual and political adherence to Rome and served as a refuge for women Cathar heretics who converted. It was expanded when Simon de Montfort, as part of the crusade against the Albigensians, entered the various

heretical strongholds of the South. He donated to the Monastery as did his men, barons from the north of the kingdom of France. By the end of the 13th century, the monastery was rich enough to make purchases and increase its land holdings.'

"I think that tells us all," I said sadly.

"The whole place," said Holmes, "was built on spoils stolen from the Cathars after they murdered them."

"And they dared to call this Monastery, Notre Dame de la Rosary; a slap in the face of those in this region who knew who Notre Dame was."

"Do you think this is where they practised torture…" I stopped abruptly as a Nun was standing in the doorway. She stepped into the room and sat down at the desk.

"Agnès de Ventadour à votre service. Je suis la prieure ici. Comment puis-je vous aider?"

We looked at each other and Holmes looked back to her and said in French that we had come to talk with the Dominican monks, Jaques and Nicolas who were recently in Paris. And asked if there were men here.

"Oui, ils sont sous la tutelle du Père Raymond, je vais l'appeler." And with that she left us alone again.

"She's gone to get Father Raymond who is in charge of the men," translated Holmes.

"Do you think she heard us?" I asked.

"No doubt but we have no idea if she speaks English."

Agnès de Ventadour returned with a rather fat priest who introduced himself as Raymond de Sales and offered us both a cigarette. Holmes took one and the cleric lit it. Holmes thanked him and thought he would try a different track. As usual I translate as best I can as the details are important.

"We are following some leads as are the Police concerning Jaques and Nicolas, who were involved in an incident in Paris."

"Yes they have been here but I was away, Sister Agnés saw them."

Holmes turned to the Prioress. "Did they see Jaques and Nicolas?"

"No," she said.

"Why not?" asked Holmes.

"They were not here."

Holmes turned to Pére Raymond "Are they here now?"

"No."

"Where are they?"

"In the Vatican," said the cleric.

"What!" exclaimed Holmes.

"Look gentlemen," said the corpulent cleric. "I was told everything by the Abbot at Narbonne and I must admit I find you quite distressing."

"Why?" said Holmes.

"You come here and almost accuse our two brothers of murder..."

"Wait..."

"No! You not only accuse our brothers but you claim there is a missing document that nobody has seen..."

I had to butt in with the best French I could muster. "We saw the beginning of the translation that Canon Lilly was making. It was an extension of a missing part of Mark 10 which said that there were these people in Jericho and..."

"Have you seen this document?" interrupted the cleric.

"No but there were two ink bottles holding it open on the dead man's desk."

The cleric turned to Holmes. "Have you seen it?"

"No I have not," replied Holmes. "Have you?"

"I have had enough of your ridiculous accusations," said Raymond angrily. "You say there is a document because there are two inkwells, that is the most ridiculous thing I have ever heard. A document nobody, you, or the police in London or the police in Paris have ever seen. This document has appeared out of thin air as nobody can tell me who owns it or where it came from. You say this ghost document adds something to Mark 10:46 *'that these people were in Jericho and Jesus met them'* which is not in any Bible, in any language whatsoever. This interview is at an end." And with that the heavy Dominican, Raymond de Sales stomped out of the room, leaving us with the Prioress in embarrassing silence.

Outside we clambered aboard the carriage and looked at each other.

"Where to?" I asked. "Rome, the Vatican?"

"There is no point now," replied Holmes. "Once the two Dominicans and the Jericho manuscript are in the Vatican they, or the manuscript are never coming out."

"You still believe there was a manuscript," I asked. "That priest made me doubt whether such a document even existed."

"It existed and he has seen it," said Holmes as he tapped to the driver. "Take us to Toulouse."

"Why Toulouse," I asked.

"We can get a diligence from there to Bordeaux."

The driver whipped up the horses and we left the Monastère de Prouilhe behind us.

"Why do you say Raymond has seen the Jericho Manuscript?" I asked.

"I can tell you a lot about that Priest and what he has been up to over the last week."

"Really, what?"

"He himself took Jaques and Nicolas and the manuscript under his supervision to the Vatican. That is why they were stalling us."

"Raymond took them?"

"Yes and he sat on the left hand side of the diligence all the way back."

I looked at Holmes waiting for an explanation. I knew he was waiting for me to ask. I didn't. After a moment we both burst out laughing. "Okay Holmes, I give in, how do you know?"

"Firstly," my good friend, "he offered us a cigarette, did you see the box, it was a Bianca, an Italian brand. Second his left wrist area was rather red compared to the right, which shows that it had the afternoon sun on it for quite some time as the coach came up from Rome along the West coast of Italy."

"What about the Jericho manuscript, how do you know he has seen it?" I asked.

"Firstly, did you notice he avoided my question as to whether he had seen it?"

"Yes but that does not really prove he has seen it."

"Wait, my very impatient friend, wait for the second point."

"I await your second point in expectation," I smiled.

"You said to him that Lilly had written an extension of Mark 10 but he replied very specifically 'Mark 10:46.'"

"Well the Abbot of Narbonne could have told him that," I said.

"Again! My, you are impetuous. I wish you would let me finish before you interrupt."

"I'm so sorry. Pray continue, the floor is yours," I bowed.

"He gave us three extra words in the manuscript" said Holmes.

I frowned. "I am so sorry to interrupt again, but what does that mean?"

"Lilly ended his writing with *'and his mother and Salome were there, and Jes...'* and Jes.... we assumed was Jesus. But our angry Raymond said it said 'these people were there and Jesus met them'."

"That's right! That's right he did say, 'Jesus met them'.

"So that angry response was just a cover," said Holmes. "A cover to make us doubt even ourselves."

I thought for a moment. "So there is no doubt that there is a Jericho manuscript and he has seen it."

"Yes he has."

"I can quite imagine a man like that using torture on anyone who dared question the accepted norm."

"I would say nowadays with torture banned they use a blank denial of anything that might throw real light on the story of the charismatic Jew called Jesus."

CHAPTER 32

Two High Priests

We hardly talked that evening in Toulouse and the mood of failure carried on the next morning as we travelled to Bordeaux and caught the train to Paris. After an hour on the train the sea came into view as the train travelled up the coast of the Bay of Biscay. There is something about the English, the sight of the sea always lifts our spirits. It certainly uplifted Holmes who started chatting away with unprovable speculations that he thought were possible given the knowledge we now had. I cannot say I took much notice as the sun passed overhead and began glistening off the sea to our left. Somehow Holmes guessed Jesus was born in 7 BC because of something written in Matthew. Then he said he suspected the story that Joseph of Arimathea came to England with Jesus was true. I said I hoped so because I loved singing Blake's 'Jerusalem'. And Holmes started singing quietly and I joined in:

"'And did those feet in ancient time walk upon England's mountains green? And was the holy Lamb of God on England's pleasant pastures seen.'"

We did not sing at full volume as the other passengers already thought we were a little strange but it was impossible not to conclude with a little extra volume.

I will not cease from mental fight;
Nor shall my sword sleep in my hand
Till we have built Jerusalem
In England's green and pleasant land.

We laughed together, then sat for a moment in silence. I looked across at Holmes. Friedrich Nietzsche had written about the Übermensch, a being who is able to completely affirm life, a superman. Is Holmes a specimen of the coming Übermensch, with his extraordinary ability to observe the most intricate of details and then remember it all and fit those details into an analysis with other new material found days later?

The train stopped at La Rochelle and Holmes could not resist another theory. It seems the Templar fleet were stationed here and when the Templars were attacked on Friday the thirteenth 1307, the fleet escaped. Holmes thought that they might have crossed the Atlantic to America, a rather unlikely tale since Christopher Columbus had not yet discovered America.

"You may not realize Watson, that you know the Knight Templar's naval battle flag."

"Do I?"

"A galleon is on the high seas;" began Holmes. "A ship is spotted in the distance. Through the telescope they recognize the flag, a skull and crossed bones! Pirates! They try to make a run for it. I ask you, why would a bunch of cut throats sit down and sow a flag with a skull and crossed bones, to warn potential prey that they are coming to rob them?"

"Now you say it, it does sound rather odd," I agreed.

"The image is based on the Knights Templars nautical battle flag. British ships probably hoisted it as they approached Spanish bullion galleons to pretend they were some of the escaped Templar fleet. Certainly Francis Drake is considered to be a pirate in Spain and in fact the city of London Guilds would finance fully gunned privateer ships as an investment. You know from our Isle of Wight adventure that the skull and cross bones, is still used in Masonic ritual today."

Speculation followed speculation as Holmes let his imagination run wild. But I must admit I was more involved with the wonderful scenery of the Loire Valley and the amazing Chateaux's that line its banks.

One speculation I do remember was that Holmes put together two pieces of information to come to a rather surprising result. Firstly that Josephus reports a strange morning light that penetrated the Holy of Holies one morning for half an hour before sunrise. Holmes guessed this was probably a conjugation of stars, probably Venus and another. Secondly that the Essene community were mainly celibate so they adopted illegitimate babies. Putting these two together Holmes thought, that with the advent of Pisces illegitimate twins, Jesus and Juda were born under the light of a conjugation. They were then considered auspicious and were adopted by the Essenes and brought up by a spiritual father, and that spiritual father was none other than Joseph of Arimathea. I quite liked that theory because the father in the Bible is called Joseph. But of course it was just wild speculation by Holmes.

The train pulled in to Gare d'Orsay and we took a cab across the river to the Place de la Concorde and then turned right to our Hotel, Le Meurice. We checked in and I complained to Holmes about the price and he again promised to pay back the Reverend Adams with his trip to the Congo.

At dinner Holmes had several books so I was not surprised that he turned to one of them once we were in the lounge, but what did surprise me was that he was confused.

"You know Watson, I have a serious problem."

"Really?"

"Remember the contradiction, that after the arrest, in the synoptic Gospels, Jesus is taken to High Priest Caiaphas, and in another Gospel he is taken to High Priest Annas and we assumed one was the High Priest who dealt with Jesus and the other was High Priest at the time of the Galilean's arrest."

"Yes that is a fair assumption," I remarked.

"I assumed Annas was the High Priest who dealt with the trial of Jesus before the Sanhedrin because of this statement in Acts." He read: *"The next day, the elders and the teachers of the law met in Jerusalem. Annas the High Priest was there, and so were Caiaphas, John, Alexander and others.'* So Annas is clearly stated to be the High Priest at this time, whereas Caiaphas is just present or inserted later. This is reinforced by the opening of Luke: *'In the fifteenth year of the reign of Tiberius Caesar, Pontius Pilate being governor of Judea, and Herod tetrarch of Galile, during the High Priesthood of Annas and Caiaphas, the word of God came to John.'* Again the title is given to Annas while Caiaphas seems to be added as an after-thought."

"I agree. So Annas is the High Priest who dealt with Jesus. So what's the problem?"

"How can I claim Annas was involved with Jesus in AD 38 when he was High Priest from AD 6 to 15? He would be a very old man in 38 AD and not High Priest."

"I see."

"Because the idea of two High Priests is so ridiculous the Church has suggested that there were not exactly two High

Priests. Annas they declare was so influential, that he was still called High Priest even after his son-in-law; Caiaphas became High Priest. So they claim one is an official High Priest, Caiaphas, and the other Annas, is an old man who was so influential, that he was still called High Priest even after he left office."

"Well," I said. That explains it for you."

"It might have helped me if it wasn't so ridiculous. Annas had five sons who were High Priests before and after Caiaphas, but low and behold, they are never, ever said to be functioning with Annas as High Priest at the same time, only with this son-in-law, Caiaphas."

"This is getting very confusing Holmes. You are worried that Annas is very old to be dealing with Jesus but then the church gives you an explanation and you don't like it."

"Too true," said Holmes. "I don't like it. But that is not the only problem with all this."

"What else is there?" I asked.

"Caiaphas was not Annas son in law and there never ever was a High Priest Caiaphas."

"What?"

"The name of the High priest at the time of Pilate was not Caiaphas it was Joseph and he was the son of Caiaphas and the son in law of Annas.

"So Caiaphas' name is really Joseph?"

"Every High Priest is called by his given name, Joshua, Simon, Jonathan, but Joseph is not! He is the only High Priest, and I mean the only one in the history of Israel, who is called by his father's name. He should be called High Priest Joseph, not Caiaphas; otherwise Jesus would be called Joseph and John the Baptist would be called Zechariah the Baptist. It is clearly nonsense."

"It does seem odd."

"Yes, and even more significantly, all mention of High Priest Joseph in Josephus' books has been changed to Caiaphas. That is really impossible because Josephus' family were high enough in the establishment to personally know Caiaphas and his son Joseph so there is no way that he would make this mistake and call Joseph, Caiaphas."

"I'm a little confused," I said. "Write down the names of the High priests and their tenure."

Holmes put his notebook on the table and starting writing the list starting with Annas son of Seth. I stood up to watch over his shoulder. I could see the sons of Annas were either side of Joseph exactly as Holmes had said.

Annus ben Seth, 6-15
Ishmael ben Fabus, 15-16
Eleazar ben Annus, 16-17
Simon ben Camithus, 17-18
Joseph ben Caiaphas, 18-
Jonathan ben Annus, 36-37
Theophilus ben Annus, 37-41

I looked at the list and looked at Holmes. "So explain your problem again," I asked.

"You can see Annus was High Priest from 6 to 15 AD yet he appears to be the High Priest dealing with Jesus. And for some inexplicable reason High Priest Joseph has been changed to High Priest Caiaphas. Why bother to do that, it makes no sense. But for some reason it is seriously important to change the name Joseph to Caiaphas, but I just can't think why."

"Give me that pencil," I said.
"What do you want it for?" asked Holmes.
"Just give me the pencil."

Holmes gave it to me and I leaned over and put two lines on the list.
Annus ben Seth, 6-15
Ishmael ben Fabus, 15-16
Eleazar ben Annus, 16-17
Simon ben Camithus, 17-18
~~Joseph ben~~ Caiaphas, 18-36
Jonathan ben Annus, 36-37
~~Theophilus ben~~ Annus, 37-41

"You see that Holmes? What they did was cut the first part of each name to leave High Priest Caiaphas and High Priest Annus."

"The bedswervers," cursed Holmes. "They have used father's names for both of them to confuse and conceal the true dates."

"So the use of the name Caiaphas instead of Joseph," I added, "is only done to be able to similarly use Annas instead of the very revealing Theophilus which would have placed Jesus alive in 38 AD exactly as you have been arguing all along."

"Watson, you are a genius!" exclaimed Holmes.

I looked at him and smiled, "Elementary my dear Holmes."

We laughed.

I went to bed that night with a glow of pride from the compliment Holmes had paid me.

CHAPTER 33

Notre Dame de Paris

In the morning we sent our cases ahead of us to Gare du Nord and after coffee walked out across the Jardin des Tuileries to the Seine. To our right was the impressive Eifel Tower.

"You know Mr. Eifel has made another spectacular that is in New York harbour. I saw it last time I was there," said Holmes.

"Yes I read about it, the Statue of Freedom," I said.

"Statue of Liberty," he corrected.

We turned left and walked along the Seine past the Louvre and crossed the Pont Neuf on to the Île de la Cité. With the Seine splitting either side of us, we walked down to the Cathedral of Notre Dame de Paris and stood outside. I had a terrible mix of feelings: anger at the theft of this spectacular building from the person the Templar architects built it for. Respect for this incredible woman who has suffered two thousand years of abuse. Hatred for those who have laid that abuse on her and replaced her with the powder puff woman, the mother. But most of all admiration and deference for the amazing Mary Magdalene. I was desperate to somehow express these feelings, and then, without thinking, I just went down on one knee and bowed my head. Holmes looked down at me and he must have been feeling the same because he went down on one knee too. We were there for maybe a minute or two without saying a word. When we finally got up we found eight tourists had taken the knee behind us, probably thinking this is what you do outside Notre Dame.

"Come," said Holmes, "lets go otherwise we will miss our train."

We crossed back to the north bank on the Pont d'Arcole. On the bridge I stopped and turned back to look at Notre Dame.

"One day," I said, 'when people know the truth, maybe they will come to Notre Dame and take the knee to the Magdalene like that."

Holmes smiled and put his arm around my shoulder and we carried on across the bridge.

"Watson," he said. "That is why I like you so much."

We caught a cab outside the Hotel de Ville and he steered straight up Boulevard de Sébastopol to Gare du Nord in plenty of time to catch our train to Calais.

On the train we reflected on the delightful journey we had had. I expressed my one regret that we did not actually get the Jericho manuscript we had set out to find. And we never got a chance to bring to justice the two Dominicans.

"Wait a minute, Watson. I know you would like a neat ending for your story with all the loose ends tied up. But the murderer of Canon Alfred Lilly has been killed and often our investigations have been brought to an end by natural justice as opposed to official justice."

"But what about the two Dominicans?"

"What was their crime? They apprehended the murderer and in the fight he died."

"But they stole the manuscript, " I pleaded.

"Stole from whom?" asked Holmes. We have no idea who owned the manuscript. For all we know Lilly might have been the original thief."

"Please don't say that to the Reverend Adams, he would be most upset."

"Of course I won't," said Holmes. "I think I like the way this has turned out. Somehow we got a taste of what has been going on for thousands of years: the editing of documents the burning of others, the denials and the lies."

"I suppose you're right. But as you say it does not make a good ending."

"My dear Watson, you are dealing with real life here, not some amateur detective story. That is why your books sell so well."

"Maybe with the title, 'Holmes takes a holiday', the readers will not expect a normal conclusion."

"What about 'Sherlock Holmes and the Hunch of Notre Dame,' à la Victor Hugo."

We laughed.

"You know what my one regret is?" said Holmes.

"No what?"

"That I never reminded Abbé Boudet to gives us his book on the Celtic language and the standing stones."

"I'm glad you forgot. What was the name of the book?"

"'La Vraie Langue Celtique et le Cromleck de Rennes-les-Bains,'" said Holmes

"Can you imagine with a name like that and the amount that man talked, I am sure the book would have been enormous."

"I'm sure it would," said Holmes. "But that Priest with his upside-down mountain and his friend with his extraordinary Magdalene Church knew a lot more than they let on. And I am sure Abbé Henri Boudet would have let slip some of it in his book."

"Terribilis est locus iste," I remembered.

The flat terrain of Picardy told us we were nearing Calais. My mind was still turning over all the things Holmes had discovered.

"Why did they hate the Magdalene so much," I asked myself. But when Holmes answered I realised I had spoken out loud.

"Paul seems to have been a fantasist and from my reading of his letters, it would not be going too far to say, Paul, and not Jesus, was the founder of Christianity. After his death in Rome, his travelling companion, Luke, sold the Romans this exaggerated story of virgin births, sons of God and resurrections from the grave. In fact Eusebius repeatedly complains about the different groups who are refusing to accept Jesus as the 'Son of God.'"

"You told me Paul never met Jesus," I remembered.

"Yes and never quotes him once in his letters. And while Jesus preached 'the sermon on the mount' Paul preached 'Christ crucified' a total misunderstanding of the process. His teachings were the real heresies and were contradicted by the teachings of Mary Magdalene and Lazarus who did know Jesus. So Luke proceeds to cut the very influential Bethany family totally from his Gospel and much of their story from Mark too. He writes the Acts of the Apostles, ignoring them and most of the Apostles and mainly tells the story of Paul who claims he is an Apostle because he was the last to see Jesus alive when he was blinded on the road to Damascus. So according to Paul, after the ascension, Jesus is supposed to have popped back down to earth, body and soul to convert Paul and make him an Apostle."

"That suggests Jesus second coming has already happened," I considered, "so we are actually awaiting his third."

"Too true," agreed Holmes. "The Bethany version of the Jesus story appears to me to be very similar to Josephus' description of Essene belief, and the Cathars could also be said to be more in tune with Essene philosophy than with the Roman Church."

"So you think there is a link between the Essenes and the Cathars?"

"Perhaps, but from what we have seen here in Cathar country, it would not be an exaggeration to suggests that what we believe now has less to do with reasoned argument, and more to do with who had the strongest and most ruthless army."

"So the Jews in Gaul had been told by the Magdalene the real beliefs of Jesus," I suggested.

"And we know what the church thought about these particular Narbonne Jews, they were *'a brothel of blaspheming Jews.'* Why are they *blaspheming Jews* as opposed to ordinary Jews? Because they believe in Jesus, but not the Jesus of the Church but the Jewish mystic Jesus? These Jews who started to escape the turmoil from as early as 40 AD would know it was Judas the Galilean whose family of fundamentalists destroyed their privileged life in Judea. They would know the Galilean was captured and killed by Pilate eight years earlier. They would know peace reigned for a while under Vitellius, till the Galilean's sons came of age and resurrected the fight. They would know how Jesus really died, as written in the Talmud. So they were clearly *'a brothel of blaspheming Jews'*. They had to be dealt with one way or another and after the Moors were cleared from Spain, the establishment began an assault on this knowledge led by Dominic Guzman and the Inquisition."

"That, I suppose, is the reason for all the scriptoriums, to doctor documents."

"And like the Jericho manuscript, to disappear others."

The train arrived at Calais and we disembarked and followed the porter and suitcase on to the quay and I sat on the bench as Holmes strolled about impatiently to await the arrival of the steamship whose smoke could be seen on the horizon.

I looked up at Holmes, "Given all the different elements you have unravelled, Chrestos, the ritual of crucifixion, the death and resurrection initiation of Lazarus, which do you think was cut from Mark 10 that was in the Jericho Manuscript."

"None," replied Holmes.

"None!" I exclaimed.

"The three women meeting Jesus in Jericho would not be the beginning of any of the revelations we have uncovered."

"There's something more that they needed to cut?"

"I believe so."

"My goodness what is it?"

"It is very much an unprovable theory as yet, so I really cannot comment on it."

I could get nothing more out of Holmes and the steamship docked and unloaded. The porter wheeled the suitcase and we followed it on to the steamship bound for Dover.

CHAPTER 34

The White Cliffs of Dover

The sea was cold and grey and I thought of our days in the blue warm sea of the Mediterranean. We went inside the cabin and ordered a cup of tea. We certainly enjoyed that tea as we had not had a descent cup since we left England.

"How can you have an upside down mountain?" I asked.

"Has that been on your mind all this time?" smiled Holmes.

"No not at all, it was just thinking of the mountains that make up the white cliffs of Dover."

"Maybe it's a major fold on top of itself and the top has worn away," suggested Holmes.

I took another sip of tea and thought about it. When I had finished, I noticed Holmes was looking at me rather strangely.

"What is it?" I asked.

"There is a theory I have had since the night of the Opera and the following day when we walked around the Pére Lachaise cemetery."

"The one in the manuscript?" I asked.

"No another," Holmes paused for a moment. "It is so strange that you might have considered me rather odd to have even contemplated it."

I could not conceive what Holmes was talking about.

"If you remember I asked what were two bigwigs doing in the tomb with Jesus?"

"Yes I remember," I said. "They were performing a ritual that would take Jesus to a higher level."

"Exactly," replied Holmes. "Now I wondered what that was because it says Nicodemus brought a mixture of myrrh and aloes, about seventy-five pounds. Do you know what these herbs are used for?"

"Of course, the healing benefits of aloe were recognized in many ancient civilization. It was used to heal wounds, relieve itching and swelling, and is known for its anti-inflammatory and anti-bacterial properties. I believe Roman soldiers carried it for emergencies"

"And myrrh?" asked Holmes.

"Yes that again," I replied, "has high antiseptic and anti-inflammatory properties. It was used to clean wounds and to prevent infection and prevent the spread of gangrene in already infected parts of the body."

"So what possible reason could there be for using that quantity of medical herbs on a dead body?" said Holmes. "There is no custom of embalming in Israel."

"Yes, so they were treating Jesus wounds," I agreed, "which proves Jesus was not dead as you have already alleged."

"Yes but that quantity?" said Holmes.

I was wondering where this was going and what it had to do with Wagner's opera and the dead bodies in Peré Lachaise.

"Do you know what the relics of Arimathea are?" asked Holmes.

"No."

"A cup to catch the blood, a reed and a sponge."

I looked at Holmes he looked at me; clearly he was hoping I could make a guess as to what he was talking about. But I had not a clue.

"Remember Wagner's Opera? Who was the bad man?"

"Klingsor."

"Klingsor, yes. Do you remember he was not worthy to join the knights who guard the Holy Grail."

"Yes."

"You are a doctor," said Holmes

"What are you getting at?" I asked.

"Look, let me read you this from Matthew 19:12 *'For there are some eunuchs, which were so born from their mother's womb: and there are some eunuchs, which were made eunuchs of men: and there be eunuchs, which have made themselves eunuchs for the kingdom of heaven's sake. He that is able to receive it, let him receive it.'* Do you receive it Watson?"

I looked down at my teacup and back up to Holmes as I began to consider the implications of what had been said.

"Are you suggesting the reed was used to keep the urethra open after an operation?"

Holmes opened Eusebius. "Perhaps this statement from Church Father Eusebius can make it clearer. *'While Origen was conducting catechetical instruction at Alexandria, a deed was done by him, which evidenced an immature and youthful mind, but at the same time gave the highest proof of faith and continence. For he took the words: 'There are eunuchs who have made themselves eunuchs for the kingdom of heaven's sake', from Matthew, in too literal and extreme a sense. And in order to fulfil the Saviour's word, and at the same time to take away from the unbelievers all opportunity for scandal – he carried out in action the word of the Saviour.'"*

"So Origen who understood the nature of Jesus and the crucifixion, seems to have cut off his phallus, and strangely after this event he became *'great and distinguished among all men...his fame increased greatly....being known for virtue and wisdom.'* Remember the visit to the cemetery to visit the tomb of Peter Abelard who also became famous after he was operated on by Fulbert, the Canon of Notre Dame, in a secret room, and the fake story of Abelard and Heloise was released."

"Are you suggesting the cup caught the blood, the read was inserted to keep the urethra open and the herbs were to disinfect the wound."

"Yes. It certainly appears so," said Holmes.

"But why would total castration be considered a move to a higher level of initiation?" I asked.

"Perhaps it involves the concept of a pure human, neither male nor female but angelic. Look at those initiated to the highest level amongst the Cathars, the true descendents of the Jesus religion. They believed that, after initiation, the Holy Spirit was able to descend and dwell within the body of the new Priest, hence the austere lifestyle needed to provide a pure dwelling place for the Spirit. So it appears Jesus by these actions became semi-angelic? So angelic, so out of this world that he says, 'Noli me Tángere'."

"You think the Cathars carried out this operation?"

"It's possible the way they talked about their Priests. But I am of the opinion that this is what Nicodemus and Arimathea were doing in the tomb."

"It does not bear thinking about," I grimaced.

"Castration was commonly performed on slaves, some eunuchs had both their testicles and phallus removed."

"In the Tacitus you gave me... or was it Suetonius, it said that when the Goddess Magna Mata was brought to Rome she was accompanied by fully castrated priests."

"In Russia, men of a devout group of Spiritual Christians known as the Skoptsy are castrated, either undergoing 'greater castration,' which entailed removal of the penis, or 'lesser castration,' in which the penis remained in place."

"Goodness gracious Holmes, I wish you had not told me."

"You are right, like what I believe was in the Jericho manuscript, I should have kept it to myself."

"Well now you have told me this theory I cannot see that what you think was in the Jericho manuscript could be any worse."

"It probably is," said Holmes shaking his head slowly.

"Oh no!"

Holmes did not answer.

"Come on, Holmes you can't just leave it like that? What happened between Jesus and these three women."

Holmes looked across at me as if I should be able to work it out for myself. I shrugged blankly. Holmes gave me a clue.

"You asked the right question."

I thought for a moment, I had asked, 'what happened between Jesus and these three women'. It slowly began to dawn on me but I did not want to put it into words. I looked up out of the window and the cliffs of Dover were looming over us.

"Blind me, Holmes we are about to land. Let's get the luggage." And I never raised the subject again.

We disembarked with a porter wheeling his case with a bump on to dry land. It was grey and it smelt different, perhaps each country has its own brand of cigarettes that pollute the air with a different smell. With Holmes' skill in identifying tobacco, I wondered if you could take him from one country to another and he would know where he was just by the smell of the tobacco.

We boarded the train for London and by the time we reached Victoria station it was dark and raining. We caught a hansom to Baker Street and we sat quietly in the dark as our horses hooves echoed on the empty streets where the gaslights glistened off the floor. We reached Baker Street and I said my goodbyes to Holmes. He slapped me on the shoulder.

"Thank you Watson, I have had the holiday of a lifetime." And with that he got out and with the help of the cabby they dragged his suitcase across the pavement and through the front door of 221B. Holmes turned and gave me a last wave and I waved back and the door closed. And from the moment that door closed Holmes never ever said another word about what he had unravelled over our remarkable journey. I think he enjoyed the fact that he, like just a few other eminent people in this world, knew the monumental secret. It gave him an even greater feeling of superiority over the rest of mankind. I on the other hand felt a burden of guilt not to be able to tell anyone, even my dear beloved.

The driver mounted the carriage and whipped the horse and I headed home to Queen Ann Street and my wife.

CHAPTER 35

The Conclusion

True to his word after a couple of weeks Holmes headed for the Belgian Congo. As I suspected it took him six days to get there and six days to get back and just two days to view the office and identify the killer as the American journalist. With the money he made he repaid every penny to my friend, the Reverend Adams.

We had several adventures together that winter and of course there were several mysterious jaunts he made to other countries at the request of high officials or nobility who would swear him to secrecy.

It was one morning in spring when I called at 221b to be welcomed as usual by a smiling Mrs Hudson, who immediately put the kettle on. I found Holmes upstairs in the parlour and he was in high spirits. We chatted over tea and he was awaiting a guest. We heard the door open below and the feet on the stairs then a knock on the door. I stood up by the bookcase to be out of the way as Holmes said "Come in Mr. Andrews." It was a young man in an expensive suit who needed help from Holmes because his father had disappeared. Holmes began in his usual manner by disarming his client with a list of observations.

"I see you walked here through Regents Park and a little early as you had time to buy some bird seed to feed the ducks."

I smiled as I watched the usual bewildered expression on Mr. Andrews' face, as Holmes continued with his detailed observations. I glanced round at the books beside me; there were the two copies of Josephus, the 'War' book and the two halves of the 'Antiquity of the Jews' now reunited again. I say two halves but luckily when one observed the split it was clear we took only one tiny part of that massive tome, and for once I was grateful the book had been vandalized, otherwise I am sure we would never have made it round France. Then to my surprise there on the shelf beside Josephus was another large book called, 'La Vraie Langue Celtique et le Cromleck de Rennes-les-Bains, by Henri Boudet.' The book on the Celtic language that Holmes wished he had taken from our friendly Priest, the *'mine of information'*. I wanted to ask Holmes how he got it, but as the subject of that journey appeared to be taboo, I waited to see if he would tell me. He never did, not then or any other time, but I slowly began to wonder if some of his secret jaunts were not for his missions impossible, but to go to Notre Dame-de-la-Mer to visit Perrine.

THE END

POSTSCRIPT

I, Julian Doyle was a close friend of Andrew Watson, the great grandson of Dr. John Watson. We came across the account you have just read nearly a year ago, amongst the reams of documents that belonged to Andrew's great grandfather. We began to research the information to see if one could throw more light, one way or the other, on Holmes's speculations. From small details for example, Andrew found reference to the review Debussy wrote on Wagner's opera, 'Parsifal' in which he wrote, *'Perhaps it is to destroy that scandalous legend that Jesus Christ died on the cross.'* To major discoveries like that made by George Andresen who noticed in the earliest eleventh century copy of Tacitus, that after the 'i' in Christians there was a gap suggesting that the text had been altered, from an 'e'.

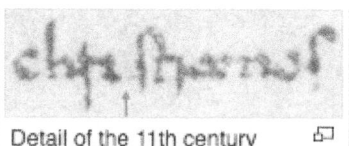

Detail of the 11th century copy of Annals, the gap between the 'i' and 's' is highlighted in the word 'Christianos'.

At first this was ridiculed as nonsense, but then using ultra-violet examination of the manuscript the alteration was conclusively shown, and Mycroft's observation was verified.

Sadly my friend was killed in a motorcycle accident, (or it is called an accident) and in his memory I continued the research that we began together. I am going to list the results later for you, which includes confirmation of the Jericho cut and the reason Holmes was reticent to discuss it.

To begin with, one general observation is that it was suggested there was a monumental secret, which Holmes's appeared to be unravelling. I tried to find any modern reference to such, other than the letter about Pousin that seemed to end up jailing Fouquet. I found an article in The Guardian, following the immanent excommunication of Archbishop Lefebvre in 1976. To their surprise the Pope suddenly backed down and they wrote:

'The Archbishop's team of priests in England, believe their leader still has a powerful ecclesiastical weapon to use in his dispute with the Vatican. No one will give any hint at its nature, but team leader Father Peter Morgan, describes it as being something 'earthshattering.' (Guardian 1976)

Those trying to fathom the mystery have, at best, come up with the story that Jesus was married and had a child, but if Holmes is right then this speculation is unlikely. Or another idea was that he had survived the crucifixion, by either being drugged or that a substitute replaced him. Again I believe Holmes makes it clear why this garbled story of a substitute exists.

Around 1628 a secret organization centred on Saint Sulpice was founded. Called the Compaignie du Saint Sacrement, to this day it is not known who was at the centre, but contemporary accounts refer to *'the secret, which is at the core of the Compaignie.'* According to one of the society's statues, discovered more recently:

"The primary channel which shapes the spirit of the Compaignie, and which is essential to it, is the secret." (Allier)

I must also mention here that together with Andrew before he was killed, we made a trip to Rome to see if there was a way of viewing the Jericho manuscript. But as expected that proved fruitless as we never got past the receptionist at the

Vatican. In researching the Dominicans though Andrew found that they were stationed in Rome in the church of Santa Sabina. We went there to see if they had any records or whether they kept any documents. Andrew pretended that he was writing a history of the birthplace of the Dominicans, Notre-Dame-de-Prouille and one of the heads was Bishop Raymond. He said it was recorded that Raymond sent a very valuable manuscript to the Dominicans in Rome. It did not work, they had no documents in the place. But it was not a totally fruitless journey because I read the pamphlet about the church and it turned out that, there was in Santa Sabina, the very first image of Jesus on the cross. We searched it out and it was a panel on an inside door high up in the top left hand corner. Andrew took two photographs one of the panel and one of me pointing to where it is on the door. I have combined them here.

Santa Sabina was consecrated in AD 440, almost exactly 400 years after the event. It is hard to believe there is no image of Jesus being crucified before this one, in any church anywhere? And even this one is strange; the crosses are not clearly represented, only two vertical posts seemingly dividing the composition into sections. It is also puzzling that the crucified figures are not attached to crosses. It seems to show that nobody had yet established a way of showing this event. But, not only were there no images of Jesus on the cross but the vertical cross was not even used by Christians as their primary image till around the Fourth century when it replaced the X cross of the Chi Rho.

It was two weeks after our visit to Rome that Andrew was killed on his motorbike by a driver who was never found.

One other thing that might interest you is that we found this tattered Bible in amongst Andrew's great grandfather's papers. Andrew believed it was his grandfather's and became shredded as he checked the references for the narrative. But I like to think it is Holmes' with his tabs and notes and the bashing it took on the journey.

Now the list for your perusal. I would ask you to remember that Holmes made his deductions using just the Bible and five books, and a couple of telegrams. The brilliance can be seen when compared with modern day research using all the tools at our disposal now.

DEATH IN 38 AD

Holmes makes a calculation that Jesus died in 38 AD. He based it on the death of John the Baptist dying after Philip died in 35 AD. There has come to light a Slavonic version of Josephus 'War' book that contains a paragraph where the Baptist talks about Philips death, making him alive after Philip died. It cannot be a Christian insertion because it contradicts the Bible story. There is also something that has slipped through the Christian censors that Holmes would not have known about. It is a statement by the church father, Epiphanius who wrote that Jesus' brother, James died in 62 AD after having been head of the church for twenty-four years. It looks an innocent enough statement in itself, which is why it has slipped through the editing process. But take twenty-four from sixty-two and it gives you the key date of 38 AD. It is accepted that, James took over the leadership after Jesus' death, but now it appears that that date is most likely 38 AD.

CRUCIFIXION AT THE START OF HIS MINISTRY

Now Holmes suggests the crucifixion occurred before Jesus took on his ministry and he quotes Eusebius' revealing attack on those who claim Jesus was crucified before Pilate came to Judea. There were several banned Gospels discovered in 1945 near the Egyptian town of Nag Hammadi. One of them, the Pistis Sophia has this: *'It came to pass, when Jesus had risen from the dead, that he passed eleven years discoursing with his disciples, and instructing them only up to the regions of the First Commandment and up to the regions of the First Mystery, that within the Veil, within the First Commandment, which is the four-and-twentieth mystery without and below.' (Pistis Sophia)*

If he died in 38 AD then according to this document, this death and resurrection event would have happened in the twenties as part of the ritual that made him a full initiate before he undertook his ministry, exactly as Homes claimed.

LUKE THE FORGER

Holmes is extremely critical of Luke suggesting he doctored the Gospels of Mark and Matthew, cutting out Lazarus and making changes that fit Paul's version of the story. Holmes also suggested it was Luke who changed High Priest Joseph to High Priest Caiaphas even in Josephus. Now, as Holmes mentioned, it is now accepted that the section about Jesus in Josephus is a forgery, although it was not considered as such at the time. Some academics believe, like Holmes, there are phrases that are not Christian, so there might well have been a mention of Jesus in Josephus. But who edited this *'Testimonium Flavianum* was impossible to say till the advent of computers. A detailed analysis of the Jesus section in Josephus by computer analysis revealed something fascinating. The first three significant nouns in the Jesus passage are the Greek words - 'Iesous, aner, ergon;' in English - Jesus, man, deeds. They then instructed the computer to perform a search of the database and look for every occurrence in the history of Greek literature of these three words, such that the words occur within a three lines of each other. The computer's output discloses an intriguing fact. There exists one passage, and only one in the whole history of Greek literature, that contains these three nouns in proximity. The matching passage is not from an obscure writer, nor was it written centuries before or after Josephus. The matching passage comes straight from the New Testament: the Gospel of Luke, chapter 24, verse 19. It was found that the correspondences between Josephus' Jewish Antiquities 18:63-64 and the Emmaus narrative of Luke show they match each other more closely than any other two Jesus descriptions to a significance level of 98%. So now the computer agrees with Holmes, Luke is the forger.

SECOND JUDAS

One of the more controversial claims by Holmes was that the second Judas was Thomas Didymus and he was Jesus' twin brother. In the jars found in the desert at Nag Hammadi, was the Gospel of Thomas, which begins,
'These are the secret sayings that the living Jesus spoke and Didymus Judas Thomas recorded.'
So Thomas as Holmes assumed, can now be confirmed as the second Judas.

In another document found, Acts of Thomas we have: *'Twin brother of Christ, apostle of the Most High and fellow initiate into the hidden word of Christ, who does receive his secret sayings.'*

The twin idea was a strong belief of Priscillian, the fourth-century teacher from Spain, who was Bishop of Avila. But in AD 386, Priscillian became the first heretic to be executed by the Church of Rome. Is it any wonder that the twin idea slowly slipped underground till it has been forgotten.

NATIVITY

Discovered in 1882, was a document called the Safed scroll. Whether it is real or fake, it states there were two brothers called Yeshai and Judas, who were the illegitimate twin sons born of a fifteen-year-old girl. I am not qualified to talk about the legitimacy of this scroll but according to it, Yeshua and his twin brother Judas, having been born illegitimately, were taken in and raised and educated by the religious order of Essene monks, with an older Essene named Joseph being assigned as Yeshai's 'religious father' and guardian. So an older Joseph was not his real father, which parallels the biblical story and supports the supposition Holmes made that Joseph of Arimathea is our man.

Now there are two points to make here, assuming the Safed Scroll is fake, it does however make it obvious that someone in 1882 had a theory about the twins. Furthermore it would be around that date of 1882 that the two statues of Joseph and Mary each holding a baby was made and placed in the Magdalene Church of Rennes-le-Château. The second point is that the Safed Scroll could have been reported in the press and Holmes could have read about it. Then, consciously or subconsciously it could have made the idea come into his head when he saw the statues. Of course that does not make it any the less real.

NOTRE DAME

Holmes claimed that Notre Dame is not Mary the mother of Jesus as is accepted now, but was the name for Mary

Magdalene. He already makes a strong case for that assumption from his visit to Notre Dame–de-le-Mer, to use its original title. But in and around 1970 books began to appear about the little church on the hill at Rennes-le-Château where the Priest was undertaking building work when Holmes and Watson visited. The claims were that he had found treasure, either Templar treasure or Visigoth treasure, to finance the work and the best seller 'The Holy Blood Holy Grail' appeared, which made several extraordinary claims, one being that there was a secret organisation behind many activities in France called, The Priory of Sion. It has been the subject of heated debate as to whether it is all a hoax or not, but the information from that book, launched another best seller, the fictional 'Da Vinci Code'. Some of the information in the books came from papers that were being deposited anonymously in the National French archives. The information related to the little church of the Magdalene in Rennes-le-Château. It gave unknown details of the Templars and also knowledge of the Cathars and the Rosicrucians that further research proved to be accurate. Amongst these secret documents is a poem in French called the Serpent Rouge, with each verse relating to a sign of the Zodiac. Leo gives us this:

From she who I desire to liberate, there wafts towards me the fragrance of the perfume, which impregnates the sepulchre. Formerly some named her ISIS, queen of the beneficial spring, COME UNTO ME ALL YE WHO SUFFER AND ARE AFFLICTED, AND I SHALL GIVE YE REST. To others she is MADGALENE, of the celebrated vase fulled with healing balm. The initiates know her true name: NOTRE DAME DES CROSS.

Genuine or fabricated, whatever the reason for its creation, this poem clearly states that those who are initiated know who Notre Dame refers to and it is *not* the Virgin Mother. Strangely the last four words are as they appear in the French, '*Notre Dame des cross*' with cross in English not the French 'croix'. And cross is singular but 'des' is pleural so it actually should translate as Notre Dame of the crosses! I can only think that the crosses is referring to the double cross of the cross of Lorraine which was a symbol used by King Rene de Anjou whose early relative was one of the initial Templars. I should add here that King Rene had a famous goblet with the words engraved on it:

"Whoever drinks from this shall see God. Whoever drinks it in one draught, will see Mary Magdalene."

One thing to remember is that Watson noted that when the two Priests and Holmes were talking in Rennes-le-Château about the painting of the Magdalene in the Cave they accidently referred to her as Notre Dame, so one can be sure they knew the significance of the heretical statues and windows they were furnishing the church with.

CHRESTOS

The extraordinary realization that the famous Tacitus statement blaming Christians for the Great Fire of Rome was actually referring to Chrestos, whom Holmes suggests is Judas the Galilean. Strangely before Holmes someone in 1770, had already made this connection. The most famous source book on the subject is, *The Decline and Fall of the Roman Empire* by Edward Gibbon and within this book he confronts the Tacitus statement about the Great Fire.

'Although the genuine followers of Moses [Jews] were innocent of the fire of Rome, there had arisen among them a

new and pernicious sect of Galileans, which was capable of the most horrid crimes.'

A pernicious sect of Galileans! Gibbon follows that statement, making it absolutely clear that, because the term Galileans had been used, Tacitus confused followers of Jesus with those of Judas:

'Under the appellation of Galileans, two distinctions of men were confounded, the most opposite to each other in their manners and principles; the disciples who had embraced the faith of Jesus of Nazareth, and the zealots who had followed the standard of Judas the Gaulonite. The followers of Judas, who impelled their countrymen into rebellion, were soon buried under the ruins of Jerusalem, whilst those of Jesus, known by the more celebrated name of Christians, diffused themselves over the Roman Empire. How natural was it for Tacitus, in the time of Hadrian, to appropriate to the Christians the guilt and the sufferings, which he might, with far greater truth and justice, have attributed to a sect whose odious memory was almost extinguished.

Gibbon had no idea that in the future Holmes would come to a similar conclusion from a very different angle, but with no axe to grind, he has unwittingly backed Holmes up by writing that those who fanned the flames of the Great Fire of Rome were called Galileans, and the person these Galileans were following was Judas the Galilean, making him the 'Chrestos' who suffered the *extreme penalty* under Pontius Pilate.

So I think we can now say more definitely that Holmes was right and Tacitus statement should read:

Chrestos [Judas the Galilean] suffered the extreme penalty during the reign of Tiberius at the hands of one of our procurators, Pontius Pilatus, and a most mischievous superstition, thus checked for the moment.' (Tacitus)

This is why Christians never quoted Tacitus as a proof of the Bible story till they had doctored it in the fourteenth century. But now Tacitus is quoted everywhere as the first non-Christian to mention the crucifixion of Jesus by Pilate. But as Holmes said, he does not actually mention Jesus at all, just someone very famous, called Chrestos an auspicious person, who suffered, 'the *extreme penalty*' at the hands of Pilate. And that person according to Edward Gibbon was Judas the Galilean.

So now there are two questions, firstly, Gibbon must have information from a source that we know nothing about. He was a member of the Royal Society, so probably a Freemason. He also lived in Switzerland and spoke French and the Grand Lodge Alpina seemed to have been involved in depositing anonymously some of the secret documents in the National French archives. So this may have been a possible source.

And secondly if he wrote this in 1770, why has it never been picked up especially as his book was standard reading in schools and colleges for a hundred years. Not only has it been ignored but Biblical experts keep repeating ad nauseam, that Tacitus statement says Pilate crucified Jesus when it does not. Is it because the church controlled education for many years? Or could it be that Biblical experts are so specialized that they don't move from the Bible and Israel into the field of Roman history? Or perhaps when anyone discovered a document that proved Jesus was alive after Pilate left Judea, he kept it to himself and his close friends because his employer was the Church and so it was not in their financial interests to disclose what they had discovered? What we can say is that all this information seems to have been known in esoteric circles for years. As Grand Master Claude Debussy wrote in his review:

"Perhaps it's to destroy that scandalous legend that Jesus Christ died on the cross."

THE DOMINICANS AND THE INQUISITION

I investigated Dominic Guzman and the Dominicans and found the encyclopaedia text for this painting by Pedro Berruguete of Dominic Guzman presiding majestically over the burning of heretics.

ST. DOMINIC PRESIDING OVER AN AUTO-DE-FE

'Representations of an auto-de-fe often depict torture or someone being burnt at the stake. The two victims in the lower right, tied to the two posts are resting on two stakes driven horizontally into the posts behind them, meant to prolong their deaths by staving off suffocation by the ropes or garrotes wrapped around their necks. Another likely purpose of these stakes was possibly a means of further shaming and humiliating the victims, due to their apparently intentional resemblance to the human male anatomy

The two victims on the posts await their deaths as the pile of ignited firewood before them is fed and fueled. The two victims standing in line await their own turns on the posts. All of these victims are Cathars, allegedly St Dominin's primary targets.'

Interestingly the encyclopaedia states at one point that the purpose of the Inquisition was to investigate *Jews who had converted* and later says it was the *Cathars who were their primary target*. Is it possible that these are one and the same and that the main drive behind Catharism was Judaism? It certainly seems a possibility.

LEONARDO AND THE FINGER

I could find no intelligent comment on the finger pointing in Leonardo paintings, but there does appear to be an answer in the supposed secret organization mentioned in the 'Holy Blood Holy Grail' called the Priory of Sion. It lists its Nautonniers (Grand Masters) some of the most famous people in history from Botticelli and Leonardo to Newton, Victor Hugo and interestingly also Debussy. I cannot tell you whether such an organization exists, or if it did whether it was called the Priory of Sion. Many have claimed it is a hoax including those who supposedly wrote it; but I cannot quite believe anyone could write a list of 26 people, which starts in 1188 and lists known and little known people who all can be shown to be interconnected and whose interconnections actually are not obvious without a great deal of research. It would be a massive undertaking just for a gag.

Jean de Gisors, (1188 - 1220)
Marie de Saint-Clair, (1220 - 1266)
Guillaume de Gisors, (1266 - 1307)
Edouard de Bar, (1307 - 1336)
Jeanne de Bar, (1336 - 1351)
Jean de Saint-Clair, (1351 - 1366)
Blanche d'Evreux, (1366 - 1398)
Nicolas Flamel, (1398 - 1418)
Rene d'Anjou, (1418 - 1480)
Iolande de Bar, (1480 - 1483)
Sandro Filipepi, (1483 - 1510)
Leonard de Vinci, (1510 - 1519)

Connetable de Bourbon, (1519 - 1527)
Ferdinand de Gonzague, (1527 - 1575)
Louis de Nevers, (1575 - 1595)
Robert Fludd, (1595 - 1637)
J. Valentin Andrea, (1637 - 1654)
Robert Boyle, (1654 - 1691)
Isaac Newton, (1691 - 1727)
Charles Radclyffe, (1727 - 1746)
Charles de Lorraine, (1746 - 1780)
Maximilian de Lorraine, (1780 - 1801)
Charles Nodier, (1801 - 1844)
Victor Hugo, (1844 - 1885)
Claude Debussy, (1885 - 1918)
Jean Cocteau, (1918 - 1963)

Anyway true or fake, these Nautonnier all take on the name John and a number (John the 21st followed by John the 22nd) But what is interesting is that the first, Jean de Gisors is John II. The writers of the Holy Blood were unsure which historical John was John the First, but they suspected it was John the Baptist. Can we now be certain that John the First was the Baptist, which explains the raised index finger in the paintings, telling us who exactly was John the number one?

Furthermore this list makes Leonardo da Vinci, who was Nautonnier between 1510 to 1519, John XIII. So is there any surprise he is selling in his paintings, his predecessor John the Baptist, as number one. As the two books Holy Blood, and Da Vinci Code have had such an influence and caused such argument about whether such an occult organization existed and whether Leonardo was part of it, I want to quote from a book written in 1978, well before Da Vinci Code, was written. The book is called 'The Hidden Art' and the author, F. Gettings wrote about occult imagery in Leonardo paintings.

'One may only speculate where Leonardo obtained his knowledge of this heretical tradition, which we nowadays relate to 'esoteric Christianity', but which even in the sixteenth century would have been quite heretical.... Perhaps Leonardo da Vinci was himself an initiate, a secret adept, and had the knowledge and had the insights from his own personal insights.'

So art historian, Gettings has spotted something in Leonardo's paintings, without any knowledge of the two later books, which does suggest something odd is going on. I should add that Debussy would be John the XXVI and would therefore also be privy to any secret information the organisation held, if it was real.

PHALLAS REMOVAL

Of the claim that Jesus had, had his phallus removed, I found no further evidence other than that which Holmes produced. There was a film though that was released in 2013 called 'Chemical Wedding' that made some interesting observation about the subject. The film mentions the Abelard and Eloise story and claims it to be a ritual exactly what Homes claimed. The film also claims a different nativity story than Holmes. It states that Joseph of Arimathea was more than Jesus' spiritual father. It quotes Eliphas Levi who was trained in St. Sulpice and wrote that: *"Elders of the line of David would impregnate a young girl to preserve the blood line."* Which suggests Joseph of Arimathea was his real father.

CHRUCIFIXION AS RITUAL

Investigating the strange idea that the crucifixion was a ritual, I, like many, I am sure, could not believe that anyone would go through with having nails hammered into their hands and feet. But then I was told that every Easter, in the Philippines, they perform a Passion play culminating with the actual nailing up of at least three penitents on to crosses. If you don't think people would crucify themselves as a ritual, then what else can one call this but a ritual.

Note that the nails are in the hands and they stand on a platform and their arms are tied to stop any pull forward putting pressure on the nails. This would be how the Jesus ritual must have looked.

ASPHYXIATION

It has been repeated over and over to me that they died of Asphyxiation. Andrew's great Grandfather already answered that point but it seems to still persist. He also suggested that the nails would have to be in the wrists to hold up the body without a platform. Well three men crucified themselves with nails through the wrist in Arizona expecting to die.

Even though they have nails in the wrist they still had to tie the hands to stop them pulling out the nails or sliding off. Trouble is these three did not die of asphyxiation or anything else. After a couple of days and nights someone called the police and the mock soldiers ran away. The victims were taken down thirsty but very much alive. Also this is supposed to be a cruel and nasty death but sightseers are out there taking selfies! So I think we can confirm what Holmes concluded about the nature of crucifixion. Andrew's great grandfather also dismissed the asphyxiation story remembering a prisoner in Afghanistan hung by his hands for days. This torture by the inquisition shows that hanging by your hands does not kill you even with weights on your feet.

So Andrew's great grandfather's story of the prisoner in Afghanistan is confirmed here.

TURIN SHROUD

I have been told several times that the Turin Shroud confirms the crucifixion of Jesus. But the shroud was used to wrap the live body of Jacques Demolay, the leader of the Knights Templar who was tortured before being burnt at the stake several years later. The shroud looks exactly like DeMolay having his long face and tall stature and Templar beard.

As the Templars did not believe in the cross, so DeMolay was scourged and then nailed to a door, as the blood from one arm is not dribbling in the direction of an outstretched arm but a raised arm. And the weight on that arm has caused it to dislocated at the shoulder, exactly what would happen if you hung from your arms awkwardly. DeMolay was then taken down alive and the shroud was placed over him. He would have owned this shroud as it is used in the Templar 'death and resurrection' ritual similar to the Masons. The body in shock produced lactic acid, ions which made a photographic image on the cloth. Biophysicist John DeSalvo suggested that lactic acid from sweat is one of those responsible for so-called Volckringer images of plant leaves, left for years between the pages of a book: substances are exuded from the leaf and react with paper fibres to produce a dark, negative image. The process suggests that the image on the shroud will slowly fade and it is doing just that. DeMolay was placed on a soft bed with his knees slightly bent so the shroud touched all of his upper body but was foreshortened from heel to the bottom, as is the shroud. Carbon dating places the manufacture of the shroud between 1260 to 1390, fitting Demolay's torture perfectly.

DeMolay signed a confession and in fact healed as the process did not kill him as nails in the hands and feet is not going to kill anyone -and when he went to trial he claimed the confession was extracted by torture. After years of deliberation, he was sentenced with his deputy, Geoffeoi de Charney to life imprisonment, but the two men recanted their confessions and that same day, a pile was erected on a small island in the Seine and there in 1314 de Molay asked to face Notre Dame Cathedral as he and de Charney were slowly roasted to death.

The family of, de Charney, the Knight burnt at the stake with DeMolay, are known to have originally owned and kept the shroud in a dark drawer where it developed. The Shroud, made its first documented appearance in 1350. At first the church was against putting the shroud on display, as they knew very well it was the image of a heretic. So it was then hidden by the Charney family for a decade before it was put on show again once the fuss of who it was had been forgotten. Now to cap it all, the shroud is supposed to prove Jesus was crucified when in fact it was created by torturing a man who did not believe in the crucifixion of

Jesus and spat on the cross. And this heretic, Jacques DeMolay was not even killed by the process, which is never going to kill anyone.

CRUCIFIXION AS A DEATH AND RESURRECTION RITUAL

I discovered this Norse Legend that may give us a clue. *'I know that I hung from that wind swept tree, nine long nights, wounded with a spear, dedicated to Oden, myself to myself, of that tree of which no man knows, from where its roots run. No bread did they give me, nor drink from a horn, downwards I peered, I took up the runes, screaming I took them, then I fell back from there."*

This is a Norse legend from the Havamal, which tells how Odin sacrificed himself on the world tree to challenge death. It ends with:

'These are the words of Odin before there were men. These were his words after his death, when he rose again.'

Odin made his spiritual journey to other dimensions of reality in his search for wisdom. He dies so as to win the occult wisdom possessed only by the dead, and rises again to use that wisdom in the world of the living. It does seem to show the type of thinking behind the ritual. You can find a similar view of initiation in Masonic text.

'He only is worthy of initiation in the profounder mysteries who has overcome the fear of death.' (The Masonic Testament)

Most importantly I found a photo of this object. It is a plaster cast, of a third century amulet and is one of the earliest images of a crucifixion even before the Santa Sabina one in Rome

One would imagine that this is the Crucifixion of Jesus. But the inscription on the amulet, reads *'Orpheus becomes a Bacchoi'*. To become a Bacchoi, is to become an enlightened disciple. So this event is an initiation. Is this what the Gnostics understood to be the crucifixion, when they said it was not to be taken literally: not capital punishment at all but a ritual of death and resurrection? This very revealing amulet has since, like the Jericho Manuscript, disappeared.

THE EDITING OUT OF LAZARUS

Andrew and I tried to trace any mention of a cut in Mark's Gospel. Andrew found that in 1958 Morton Smith, a professor of ancient history at Columbia University, discovered a letter in the Monastery of Mar Saba, situated twelve miles outside Jerusalem. The letter was written by the second century church father, Clement of Alexandria. Here is the opening salvo, an unabashed encouragement to tell lies.

'To Theodore. You did well in silencing the unspeakable teachings of the Carpocrations.... Such men are to be opposed in all ways and altogether. For, even if they should say

something true, one who loves the truth should not, even so, agree with them. For not all true things are the truth, nor should that truth which merely seems true according to human opinions be preferred to the true truth, that according to the faith.'

So lie if you have to, to preserve the Jesus story coming from Rome. He then describes Mark and his Gospel.

'As for Mark, during Peter`s stay in Rome he wrote an account of the Lord`s doings.... But when Peter died a martyr, Mark came over to Alexandria, bringing both his own notes and those of Peter, from which he transferred to his former books the things suitable to whatever makes for progress toward knowledge. Thus he composed a more spiritual Gospel for the use of those who were being perfected. Nevertheless, he yet did not divulge the things not to be uttered, nor did he write down the hierophantic teaching of the Lord, but to the stories already written he added yet others and, moreover, brought in certain sayings of which he knew the interpretation would, as a mystagogue, lead the hearers into the innermost sanctuary of truth hidden by seven veils. Dying, he left his composition to the church in verso Alexandria, where it even yet is most carefully guarded, being read only to those who are being initiated into the great mysteries.'

The important aspect of this is that the letter clearly states that Jesus is a *'hierophant'*, which is an interpreter of sacred mysteries or esoteric principles. And a mystagogue is someone who instructs others before initiation into religious mysteries. The letter now mentions two sections of Mark's Gospel that had been cut out. One very large section that Clement states was between verses 34 and 35 of Mark 10 turns out to be, the story of the raising of Lazarus. So this confirms Holmes belief that Lazarus was cut from the synoptics. It begins with a very recognizable trait.

'And they come into Bethany. And a certain woman whose brother had died was there.

You will recognise this *"a certain woman"* nonsense? I am sure Mark would not have been so coy with the names, but we can identify this trait as being *'a certain man's* handiwork, or at least someone with the same problem as Luke, with the names of those in Bethany. So this clearly has been edited first to remove the names of Lazarus and his sister, Mary, but then they decided they just could not stomach any of it, so the whole lot was cut out. It continues.

And, coming, she prostrated herself before Jesus and says to him "Son of David, have mercy on me." But the disciples rebuked her. And Jesus, being angered, went off with her into the garden where the tomb was, and straightaway a great cry was heard from the tomb. And going near Jesus rolled away the stone from the door of the tomb. And straightaway, going in where the youth was, he stretched forth his hand and raised him, seizing his hand. But the youth, looking upon him, loved him and began to beseech him that he might be with him. And going out of the tomb they came into the house of the youth, for he was rich. And after six days Jesus told him what to do and in the evening the youth comes to him, wearing a linen cloth over his naked body. And he remained with him that night, for Jesus taught him the mystery of the kingdom of God. And thence, arising, he returned to the other side of the Jordan.' (Secret Mark)

Let us take this bit-by-bit.

'And straightaway, going in where the youth was, Jesus stretched forth his hand and raised him, seizing his hand.

The emphasis on, *seizing his hand,* sounds like the magic grip used to raise the novitiate in Freemasonry. Here is a symbolic representation of a Masonic resurrection from the grave, using the Lion's paw grip, and taking place in Ancient Egypt, suggesting an ancient origin of the ritual.

Just for you information here is the Lion's paw, Master Mason grip.

So does this explain the disciples statement *"Let us also go, that we may die with him?"* So that we can be born again as an initiate.

Now continuing:

But the youth, looking upon him, loved him and began to beseech him that he might be with him. And going out of the tomb they came into the house of the youth, for he was rich. And after six days Jesus told him what to do.' (Secret Mark)

That seems to confirm that Jesus is a Hierophant initiating the novice into secret knowledge.

'and in the evening the youth comes to him, wearing a linen cloth over his naked body. And he remained with him that night, for Jesus taught him the mystery of the kingdom of God.'

I am having real trouble thinking of an innocent interpretation of this event between Jesus and Lazarus. Does this suggest that Lazarus is the 'disciple Jesus loved' literally? Perhaps you could argue that this seemingly lurid association was never in the Gospel, but luckily the youth appears later in our present day Mark, using the same Greek word *'neaniskos'* for him reinforcing the fact that this Lazarus story was once in Mark. This is from the arrest of Jesus?

'A young man, wearing nothing but a linen garment, was following Jesus. When they seized him, he fled naked, leaving his garment behind.' (Mark 14:51)

I think we can be safe to say the raising of Lazarus was in Mark's Gospel, but first the names were edited out (which does suggest Luke's handiwork) and then the whole event was removed at an early date. But when John's Gospel was incorporated into the Bible the problem with Bethany seems to have been solved (or perhaps Luke is dead now) and the Church felt able to mention Lazarus.

THE JERICHO MANUSCRIPT

Now we come to the second cut in the Gospel of Mark as mentioned in the Clement letter above. To our surprise and anticipation it is the Jericho cut! We had high hopes that it would reveal the contents of the Jericho manuscript. But he writes:

'After the words, "And they came to Jericho," the secret Gospel adds only, "And the sister of the youth whom Jesus loved and his mother and Salome were there, and Jesus did not receive them".

Adds only!! Somebody cut the text to leave this nonsense, where Jesus arrives in Jericho, these people are there, but he didn't see them! It is ridiculous. Why would they need to cut that? But in fact the Bishop Raymond gave us a clear sign that it is not true because he added the words 'met them'. So it should at least read "*And the sister of the youth whom Jesus loved and his mother and Salome were there, and Jesus met them!* So we are still stumped as to what happened in Jericho because if Clement can't even repeat it, it must have been very revealing.

Holmes suggested something sexual occurred between Jesus and at least one of the women. He never gave us a clue as to why he thought this but he may have been right. Clement's letter is addressed to a Theodore, who seems to have been told by a group called the Carpocrations, that there is more. Clement's letter starts:

To Theodore. You did well in silencing the unspeakable teachings of the Carpocrations. For these are "wandering stars" referred to in the prophecy, who wander from the narrow road of the commandments to a boundless abyss of the carnal and bodily sins.

Carnal and bodily sins does suggest something sexual. Our only record of the Carpocratians, comes from Christian critics. who declare them as mystic Gnostics. It appears here that they are quoting the secret Gospel of Mark to justify their carnal activities. Christian sexual rites may sound strange nowadays, but a heretical group, 'the Bulgari' had their name associated with sodomy by Catholic propagandists, and 'bugger' is still in use today. Obviously the Carpocratians were quoting something odd going on in Jericho, and Clement is denying it. Instead he gives us this nonsensical section that, *at Jericho there were these people who Jesus never met!* Could the Carpocrations have seen the full original text of the Jericho cut that included something explicit going on in Jericho? Well it is accidently made clear by Clement that they did:

'[Mark] brought in certain sayings of which he knew the interpretation would, as a mystagogue, lead the hearers into the innermost sanctuary of truth hidden by seven veil...., he left his composition to the church in Alexandria, where it even yet is most carefully guarded, being read only to those who are being initiated into the great mysteries.'

Clement now admits that the leader of the Carpocrations, one Carpocrates, has seen it.

'But since the foul demons are always devising destruction for the race of men, Carpocrates, instructed by them and using deceitful arts, so enslaved a certain presbyter of the church in Alexandria that he got from him a copy of the secret Gospel, which he both interpreted according to his blasphemous and carnal doctrine.'

Holmes was right, something really carnal was in the Jericho Manuscript.

This letter by Clement is vitally important to Biblical studies and luckily, it was photographed by Prof. Morton Smith in black and white and then by some of his students who visited Mar Saba and took colour photos. But any further attempts to see the letter have failed and it has, like the Jericho manuscript, not only disappeared but since the death of the Professor, he has come under a series of attacks and accusations of actually manufacturing the letter himself. So I presume Holmes' will suffer the same abuse in the future and his revelations will be forgotten.

> But as Sherlock Holmes used to say, "once you eliminate the impossible, whatever remains, no matter how improbable, must be the truth"

To 'Whispering' Paul McDowell
Whose spirit guided my fingers over the keyboard

JULIAN DOYLE TAKES THE KNEE

Photo. Sukanya Panyamat

ABOUT THE AUTHOR

JULIAN DOYLE is the editor of 'Life of Brian' and is also one of the world's most versatile filmmakers. He has written and directed his own films, and edited, photographed and created Fx on others. He is most famous for editing the Monty Python Films and shooting the Fxs for Terry Gilliam's movies 'TimeBandits and 'Brazil', which he also edited.
He has written and directed three feature films. 'Love Potion' about a drug rehabilitation centre, described as Hitchcockian. 'Chemical Wedding' featuring Simon Callow about the outrageous British occultist, Aleister Crowley and described by one American reviewer as 'Thoroughly entertaining although at times you wonder if the film makers have not lost all there senses'. He has also directed award winning pop videos such as Kate Bush's 'CloudBusting' featuring Donald Sutherland and Iron Maiden's 'Play With Madness'.

He recently wrote and directed the play 'Twilight of the Gods' investigating the tumultuous relationship between Richard Wagner and Friedrich Nietzsche and described by 'Philosophy Today' as 'Masterful!' Python's, Terry Jones has described him as an original Polymath.

Julian was born in London and started life in the slums of Paddington. His Irish father, Bob, was one of the youngest members of the International Brigade that went to fight against Franco's invasion of democratic Spain. His mother, Lola, was born in Spain of an Asturian miner who died early of silicosis. She was thereafter brought up in a Catholic orphanage in Oviedo.

Julian started his education at St. Saviours, a church primary school. He went on to Haverstock secondary school, one of the first comprehensive schools in England. His first job was as a junior technician to Professor Peter Medawar's team, which won the Nobel Prize soon after Julian's arrival. Not that he claims any credit for that. At night school he passed his 'A' level exams and took a Zoology degree at London University. After a year at the Institute of Education, he taught biology before going to the London Film School. On leaving he started a film company with other students. Besides film making, Julian is well known for his Master-classes in Film Directing.

While still at school, Julian had a daughter, Margarita who was brought up in the family. He then had two further children, Jud and Jessie.

Clearly, Julian Doyle is a very naughty boy!

ALSO BY JULIAN DOYLE

THE GOSPEL ACCORDING TO MONTY PYTHON

Who was the real Brian?
Who was the real Jesus?
Who was the real Bishop of Southwark?
Did the Romans build the Jerusalem Aqueduct?
Were the Magi wise?
Was Brian's father Nortius Maximus, and
Were the Peoples Front of Judea, really splitters?

All the crucial issues this book dares to confront.

With a FORWARD by TERRY JONES

And a BACKWARD by MICHAEL PALIN

Available from all good bookshops

Amazon US   https://www.amazon.com/dp/1981903569
Amazon UK   https://www.amazon.co.uk/dp/1981903569

Printed in Great Britain
by Amazon